QUICKLY,
BEFORE ALL THE
REST OF THEM DO,
FOR HERE AND
FOR THERE
HE HAS LEFT CLUES
BEHIND HIM,
VERY WELL SHOWING, EXPRESSLY
FOR YOU.
UNDER SKIES THAT ARE
AZURE AND SKIES THAT
ARE BLACK,
COME ALONG! YOU AND I!
LET'S BRING APPLEBY
BACK!

The Story of Appleby Capple

THE STORY OF
APPLEBY CAPPLE

WRITTEN AND ILLUSTRATED BY

Anne Parrish

HARPER & BROTHERS   PUBLISHERS   NEW YORK

FOR DILLWYN PARRISH

Late one night, in winter, in snowy December,
    We started this story, telling it to each other.
Fire was warm and roses smelled sweet, I remember,
    And we whispered, so that we wouldn't waken mother.

Out in the hall the grandfather clock was ticking,
    Petals fell, and the ashes ran with red.
And we heard the wind, and sleet on the windows clicking,
    And mother called to us, "Children, come to bed!"

"We'll go on with the story tomorrow—we'll do it together."
    Then we had to go back to our lessons; it didn't get done.
And time has drifted past like a wind-blown feather.
    But wasn't it fun, little brother? Wasn't it fun?

The Story of Appleby Capple

A

Here is a boy named Appleby;
Apple, he's called for short.
A friendly child, as all agree,
And very fond of sport.

Apple may seem an odd name—not odd for a fruit, but odd for a boy. Yet it is not a bit more unusual for a boy than Banana, Tangerine-Orange, Pineapple, or Choke-Cherry would be. I have never heard of any boys with those names, but there are a great many things I have never heard of; I have heard of three boys who lived in the jungle in Africa who were called Newspaper, Primrose, and Cup-of-Tea. Their father and mother had been taught to read English, and chose the prettiest names they could find for their little sons.

But let us go back to Apple.

Appleby Capple is visiting his aunts and uncles and cousins, Aunt Bella and Uncle Francis, Aunt Ella, Cousin Kate and Cousin Lucy, and Cousin Clement. He goes from one house to another, has a toothbrush in every house, and is welcome everywhere.

He is now on his way along a lane to tea with his Aunt Bella, to celebrate the birthday of his Cousin Clement, who is ninety-nine years old today.

Apple is troubled, because he has not yet found a birthday present for Cousin Clement. He knows what he wants it to be. What Cousin Clement likes best in the world is to look at butterflies—not to catch

1

them—to look at them and paint them in water colors. He has painted so many different kinds that the walls of his house, where he has pinned his paintings, seem to be made of butterfly wings. There are paintings of wings colored like the sky, the sea, the sun, the moon, leaves, fire, marigolds, black night, snow, bark, mother-of-pearl, feathers, dust, lilacs, and the bright green-yellow of mustard flowers. There are pale green wings edged with deep purple, gleaming more silkily than thistledown, black velvet wings streaked with bright yellow lightning or clouded with pale blue. There are cinnamon and silver wings splashed and veined with scarlet. Enough wings to satisfy anyone, you and Apple and I might think. But Cousin Clement thinks otherwise.

"Appleby, my boy," he said one day when the two were painting together, and the paint water in their glasses was getting muddier and muddier, and they had forgotten long ago not to put their brushes in their mouths to make fine points, although Aunt Bella, Aunt Ella, Cousin Kate, a friend of the family named Mr. Rollo Roberts, and Caleb, Cousin Clement's coachman, often reminded them that this is a very bad habit—what *was* I talking about? Oh, it was Cousin Clement who was talking.

"Appleby, my boy, in me you see a miserable failure. True, I have seen millions of butterflies. But in all the ninety-eight years, eleven months, twenty-five days, fourteen hours, and—" he pulled out his watch—"twelve minutes and three seconds of my life, I have never seen a Zebra. Have you?"

"Yes, Cousin Clement, I have!"

"You have? I am proud of you! Allow me to shake your hand."

Apple allowed Cousin Clement to shake his hand.

"It was, of course, deep black, with stripes of—"

"White."

"White! You have discovered a new species! In time it may be named for you! Heliconius Applebius! I am proud to be your cousin, sir! I have only heard of yellow stripes, three on the upper wing, one on the lower—"

2

Apple picks an Arethusa for Aunt Bella. The butterfly over it is an
Admiral, and the butterfly over the Arrowhead plant is an Aurora.
Not a Zebra butterfly in sight.

"My Zebra didn't have wings."

"No wings?"

"It had four legs—"

Cousin Clement sighed and collapsed, like a balloon when the air leaves it. He said in a small, discouraged voice, "I was talking about a butterfly called the Zebra."

"Oh—"

"Perhaps you know it as Heliconius charitonius? Would you prefer me to use the Latin name?"

"No, thank you, Cousin Clement, thank you very much."

3

"The Zebra, then. So neither of us has seen it, after all."

"No, Cousin Clement."

"I have kept pots of passion flowers by open windows, for they are the Zebra's favorite food. I have listened for creaking in every cocoon I find, for the Zebra can creak and squeak while it is still wrapped in its cocoon. I have traveled the world over—no Zebra. I have failed."

He sighed so hard that the picture of the Aurora butterfly that he was painting flew out of the window, as though its orange-tipped yellow wings were real.

Then and there Apple decided that somehow the sight of the Zebra must be his birthday present to Cousin Clement.

Now it is the afternoon of Cousin Clement's birthday, and Apple has not found a single Zebra.

But he has not yet despaired, and, still searching, he leaves the lane to gather a few flowers to take to Aunt Bella, going deeper into the wood, following a stream that flows into a swamp where arrowheads grow, and gathers an arethusa.

Perhaps you call it swamp pink—many people do. Perhaps you don't call it anything—many people don't.

Fortunately, Apple has worn his new rubber boots.

Except for an Adjutant Bird, he seems to be alone, but the Adjutant Bird would not be there unless frogs, fish, and snakes were there, too. And there is quite a lot of the adjutant bird to be with Apple, for he is six feet tall (the adjutant, not Apple). His other name is marabou stork. Apple's Cousin Lucy has a pretty bed jacket edged with downy pink marabou feathers, and if anyone had told Apple that he was looking at the kind of bird they came from, he wouldn't have believed it, for adjutants are not downy, pale-pink birds, but plain indeed, with enormous beaks, sharp eyes, long bare necks, and bald heads. It is the down hidden under their tail feathers that is gathered and dyed pretty colors. This one that we are looking at still has all his down, and I, for one, wouldn't want to try to take it from him.

Something hits Apple, and he would have jumped, except that his

4

An acorn hits Apple, an Arrow flies through the air, an Adjutant Bird approaches, and Apple is alarmed.

5

boots are too deep in the ooze of the swamp. It is only an acorn. Perhaps a chipmunk threw it at him; perhaps an oak tree threw it.

Suddenly an Indian arrow flies through the woods and lies at his feet.

Apple wishes that he were in armor, like a knight of old, but he always tries to be a brave boy, and quite often is, and he picks up the arrow. It will be better than nothing for a birthday present.

"Only I wish I could find the Zebra. And that reminds me, I must

Apple wishes that he were in Armor.

6

be on my way to the party," Apple says, to himself, for the adjutant bird has disappeared, stalking stiffly away like an officer on parade—indeed, like the adjutants he is named for, who are staff officers in the army.

Apple has to hold onto a willow to pull his boots (with his feet in them, of course) out of the swamp. Each comes with a sound like a long s-u-c-k and a loud SMACK. Then, on solid earth once more, he thinks, Where am I?

He cannot follow the sun; a cloud has come over it.

"The stream led me in, it will lead me out," he tells himself.

But seven small streams run into the swamp, and which is Apple's stream?

He wonders whether anyone has missed him.

If I had a carrier pigeon, I could send a message, he thinks. If I had some balloons, I could let them up to show the world outside the woods where I am.

He thinks he is alone in the swamp—but is he?

Is that the wind in the leaves, or is it a stealthy footfall?

Is that a dead stick lying on the ground, or did it just give a wriggle?

Whose are those eyes looking down from a tree?

And is that a mossy old log lying in the water, or is it something else?

And Apple thinks he will find his way back, but will he? He has gathered a flower and found an arrow in safety—but he still has to get out of the woods.

B

Apple's Aunt Bella now we see,
And Bob, her birdie dear.
"Now where," she asks, "can Apple be?
It's time that he was here!"

Aunt Bella has baked a beautiful birthday cake, decorated with icing butterflies to please Cousin Clement and blush roses to please herself, for Cousin Clement's ninety-ninth birthday, and asked Apple to help blow out the candles and eat the cake. One hundred candles— for, of course, there is one to grow on—take a lot of blowing.

"If they don't come soon the birthday cake will spoil their suppers," she says to birdie Bob, and Bob answers, "Tweet! Tweet!" and bursts into song.

Her other pets—she and her husband, Uncle Francis, have a great many—are somewhere. The crested cockatoo that Cousin Clement gave her for Christmas is on his perch under the cherry tree, eating cherries. I don't know where pug Quentin and cat Pussy are at the moment. As for Nanny the goat, no one ever knows where she will appear next.

How peaceful it is in Aunt Bella's parlor, with the late afternoon sun streaming through the windows, shining on the blossoming bulbs, the bunch of bluebells, and the fat blue Chinaman on the teapot. He is so fat that he must have drunk a great many bowls of bird's-nest soup and eaten a great many hundred-year-old eggs, great delicacies in

8

Aunt Bella brings in the Birthday Cake. Brioche, butter-balls, and a teapot painted with a Blue Chinaman are on the table. Aunt Bella's bulb is blooming, and her bird in his bird-cage bursts into song.

China, as I'm sure you know, **and** he wears a hat like a blue mushroom and is smoking a long blue pipe with a curly pig's tail of blue smoke coming out of it. Not only is his hat blue, and his sash, and his fan, but his face. Blue nose, blue eyebrows, blue everything.

I like blue, but I would not care for a blue face, would you?

The sun gilds the big birthday cake, too, and the brioche and the butter balls, and the honey.

Bees make honey; I know you know that, but if I only tell you things you don't know, I won't have much to tell you.

Bears like to eat honey (you know that, too), and they hunt for combs of wild honey in hollow trees and, having no finger bowls or napkins, always lick their paws clean after the feast. Bears are tidy when

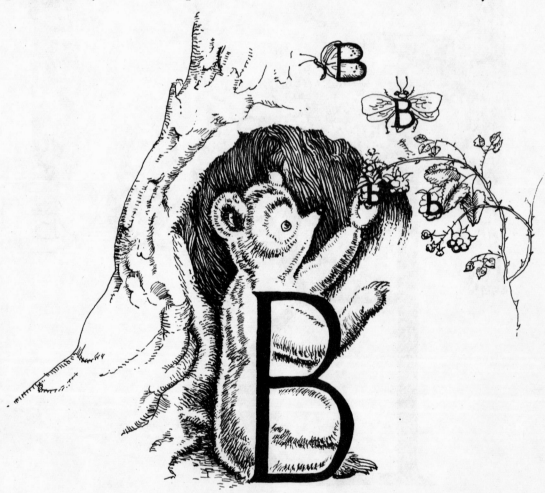

A Bear eating blackberries sees a Bee, and hopes for honey. The butterfly isn't a Zebra, it is the kind called a Bright Blue.

10

they eat. I have seen a mother bear and her two cubs carefully peeling oranges before eating them; one cub tried to cram the whole orange into his mouth, but his mother gave him a good hard spank, and then he peeled his orange, too.

Bears also like blackberries.

Speaking of bears, Apple (who likes honey, oranges, and blackberries, and is growing so hungry that he would welcome even oatmeal or string beans) thinks he has just seen a bear, though perhaps it is a shadow in a wind-shaken bush. He does see a bee, and some green blackberries that he tries to eat, but he cannot swallow.

Then he sees something else. His hair rises, his teeth chatter.

What does he see?

And what is looking at him that he does not see?

C

A Caterpillar from behind
A leaf looks on the stranger
With interest both mild and kind
And not a thought of danger.

The caterpillar is called Caterpillar, and has no other name, any more than a daisy or a pebble has. Caterpillars are caterpillars, and never so far forget that fact as to invent names such as Gaily or Campbell or Freddie for each other.

Caterpillar hasn't been doing much or thinking much; he hears the seven sounds of the seven streams, each different but making one music together, and the chirping of a flock of birds talking among themselves without making any effort to keep their voices down, just as though they were the only creatures in the tree, or in the world. Caterpillar likes not being noticed; he is quiet by nature, and modest. He lies under one leaf and on another, eating a green mouthful now and then, hearing the brooks and the birds.

Now he hears new sounds, a squish-squish and a sigh, and looks down on Appleby in the rubber boots full of mud, water, and small specimens of swamp life.

Caterpillar is so interested that he forgets to swallow the scrap of leaf hanging from his mouth and stretches himself out from under the shelter of the leaf above him. He does not notice the crow launching down from the clouds.

Neither does Apple, for exactly at this moment the mossy old log in the swamp water opens its mouth.

It is a crocodile.

Apple yells and jumps, frightening the crow away from Caterpillar, who, eyes huge with terror, has just seen it.

He is so grateful to Apple for saving his life that he promises himself he will do anything, everything, to show his gratitude.

The same thought occurs to a fish, who was trustfully swimming toward the crocodile-log, and now swims away as fast as she can flip her fins.

She is a tiny fish, and her name is Common Silverside, so that is what we will have to call her, even though it doesn't sound very polite. You could hunt through all the streams and never find a kinder little creature, and now, like Caterpillar, Common Silverside is grateful to Apple for saving her life and is determined to save his, for she knows the danger he is in.

She swims up the stream trying to find the next-kindest person to Apple that she has ever met—a fisherman who has caught her so many times and put her back in the water so many times that they have become firm friends. She knows he will help her hero.

12

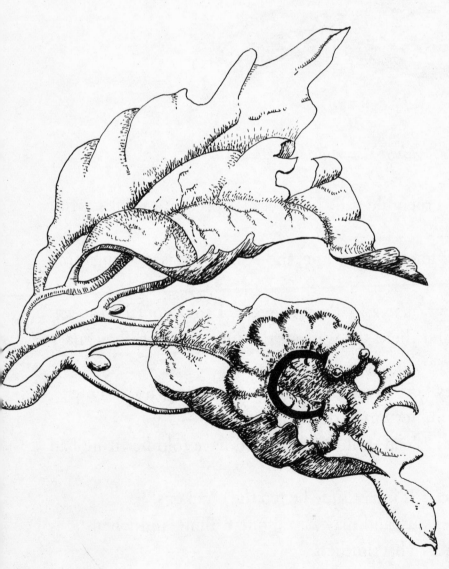

Caterpillar does not see a dangerous Crow.

13

Common Silverside sees Crocodile.

Meanwhile, the crocodile rolls his eyes at Apple and thinks, Must be about suppertime.

And indeed it is almost suppertime, and Aunt Bella is growing more and more anxious.

"Where are they?" she asks Pussy the cat. I told you the cat was somewhere about, and there she was, all the time, making the canary nervous.

"Where can they be?" Aunt Bella asks the canary (who, of course, is our old friend, Bob, her birdie dear).

But the canary is asleep; not that he could have told her if he had been awake.

"Where is Francis? It is past time he fed the chickens."

She fears that her husband may have gone fishing, and when he is fishing he never notices what time it is.

"Where is Ella?"

14

The Chickens hope that Cockatoo, on his perch where convolvuluses (or morning-glories) climb, will drop his cherries.

15

Apple's Aunt Ella is Apple's Aunt Bella's twin sister. Aunt Bella sent an invitation to the birthday party to Aunt Ella by Uncle Francis, together with a basket of fresh-laid eggs from Uncle Francis' chickens, and Uncle Francis remembered to give Aunt Ella the eggs but not the invitation.

Aunt Ella, with cries of thanks and delight, put the eggs in a bowl, filled the basket with just-gathered strawberries from her garden, and gave him an invitation to take back to Aunt Bella, for the sisters each had the same idea about a birthday tea for Cousin Clement.

But Uncle Francis forgot that note, too.

Let us return to poor bewildered Aunt Bella.

First she feeds the chickens.

Then she goes for Cockatoo, who is enjoying the air and almost too many cherries under the cherry tree.

When Cousin Clement gave Cockatoo to Aunt Bella for Christmas, his sharp beak, his eyes as red as currants, and his harsh screams (Cockatoo's, of course, not Cousin Clement's—Cousin Clement has kind brown eyes behind large spectacles, a nose that is simply a nose, and a quiet voice that he doesn't use much) frightened Aunt Bella a little. But now they love each other dearly. At sight of her, Cockatoo dances and prances from side to side of his perch, lifts his snow-white wings to show their bright pink linings, raises the white, scarlet, and yellow-banded feathers of his crest, and screams for joy. As he rides to the

⟶   *Aunt Bella has gone to look for the company that doesn't come. Here is her empty chair, with Pussy the Cat in front of it, and Uncle Francis' chair with the Canary asleep on it. On the mantelpiece are the conch-shells, the cup of cold tea, with another Chinaman on it, the clock that doesn't go, and a photograph of Cousin Clement playing croquet. The butterfly behind him is a Claudia. The cuckoo in the cuckoo clock is telling the wrong time, and the Christmas-present calendar is telling the wrong month and year, because Aunt Bella is too fond of the robin singing a Christmas Carol to change it. Over the mantelpiece is a Queen at her Coronation, with her Crown, her hair in a chignon and corkscrew curls, and the Crinoline she forgot to cover.*

16

house on her shoulder, he leans gently against her cheek and tries to tell her all about his afternoon.

Aunt Bella usually answers, whether she understands or not, but now she is too worried.

She tries to calm herself with a cup of tea, but it is cold.

Neither the clock on the mantelpiece nor the cuckoo clock give her any comfort. One stopped years ago, and the other is cheerful but unreliable, and often cuckoos as many as seventeen times at once, and sometimes more.

By the way, the conch shells on each side of the mantelpiece clock and the curious corals in the cabinet are gifts from Great-Uncle Thomas, a seafaring man, who brought them back from tropical seas. He loves to give presents, and has often had to hire a caravan of camels to carry the keepsakes he collects to bring home to his relatives.

Aunt Bella loves the conch shells and the coral; she loves the mantelpiece clock, even though it won't tell time. She loves the picture over it, of a queen at her Coronation, and enjoys hearing callers cry, "How unusual!" For the queen has her crown on top of her chignon and corkscrew curls, and has remembered her scepter and her ermine robe, but has forgotten to put her skirt on over her crinoline. I suppose nobody dared remind her; it probably isn't polite to say to a queen, "Mercy, Your Majesty! Put on your skirt!" So there she stands in her crinoline and her pantalets, poor thing, and Aunt Bella loves her.

Aunt Bella has a very loving heart, and usually a cheerful one, but now it is anxious and heavy.

"And where can Cousin Clement be?" she sighs.

Probably hunting butterflies, she thinks, and, if he is, there is no telling when he will remember anything else. Once he and Aunt Bella were playing croquet, and he went after a ball she hit through a hedge, and didn't come back for a week, because he saw a butterfly and followed it. Nobody knows what became of the mallet he was carrying when he crawled through the hedge. It was the one with the orange

18

A Camel Caravan carrying a cargo of curios. "Come on!" the Cameldriver is crying to Caliph, the leading camel. The other camels are called Cairo, Cadi, Cush, Cheops, and Cook's-Tours, all well-known names in Egypt.

19

band, and, after that, the person who played with the orange ball had to borrow a mallet for every stroke.

Now, clasping her hands in distress, while a tear splashes into her cold tea, Aunt Bella cries, "Where is Apple?"

But let us go back to Cousin Clement, back, that is, to what I can tell you about him, for I don't know any more than you or Aunt Bella do where he is at this moment.

Cousin Clement lives in a big old house, alone except for old Caleb, who is companion, caretaker, cook, coachman, cleaning man, and—his favorite occupation—carnation grower. "And complainer!" Cousin Clement tells him, when Caleb complains of being bothered by butterflies. For when the weather grows cold, Cousin Clement gathers cocoons and puts them in his conservatory, and the butterflies, when they come out, think it is summer, although snow may be falling outside.

Caleb says butterflies bother him; he is tired of trying to pick a flower and having it fly away.

"And cocoons all over my carnations," he complains.

But he is careful to be in the conservatory when Cousin Clement is painting butterflies. Sometimes when he is pleased with a picture, Cousin Clement will say, "Dear me! How stupid I am! This blue isn't a bit like the butterfly's blue," or, "I'm afraid I've made a mess of this delicate veining," hoping that Caleb will say, "It's exactly the right color," or, "You never went over the edge at all. I don't see how you do it so beautifully."

But Cousin Clement gets no compliments from Caleb.

No wonder Cousin Clement enjoys the hours when Apple paints with him and thinks everything Cousin Clement paints is wonderful, and says so out loud.

No one knows what Caleb thinks, but he always looks at the pictures, pretending not to, and often is so interested that he waters Cousin

Cousin Clement painting in the conservatory, and hoping for a compliment from Caleb. You can see a Christmas fern, a centifolium lily, campanulas and carnations, and nineteen butterflies, Crescent-spots, Calicoes, and Camberwell Beauties. The ones among the flowers are rather difficult to find, and so is the cocoon hanging from the center carnation plant.

21

Clement instead of a cyclamen, a calla lily, or his own cherished carnations.

In the conservatory just now the butterflies are, to the best of my knowledge, mostly the Crescent spots, the Crimson patches, and the Calicoes, both the white-skirted and the orange-skirted, of course. Please correct me if I am wrong.

Apple loves the conservatory, and spends happy hours there, seeing how some of the butterflies can almost vanish simply by closing their bright wings so that only the dead-leaf-colored lining shows, or how they uncoil tongues finer than hairs and coiled like watchsprings, to thrust into the tubes of flowers, in search of honey.

On the afternoon of his birthday Cousin Clement started for Aunt Bella's party and Aunt Ella's party, for both invitations had come to him through the kindness of Mr. Perkins the postman. He was delighted to be going to two parties in one day; such a thing had never happened to him before. He expected each lady to surprise him with a birthday cake.

"But if I can't manage two pieces, Appleby will be there, and Appleby will eat them for me," he told himself.

Caleb drove him in the calash. And, on the way, Cousin Clement caught sight of a butterfly that might be—just *might* be—a Zebra. Out he jumped and off he went into the woods.

He said he would be gone only a minute, but you remember what happened when he was playing croquet with Aunt Bella.

Aunt Bella! What with talking about cocoons and carnations and compliments—not to mention cake—I'd forgotten all about poor Aunt Bella crying into her cold tea and wondering where Apple is.

Apple is wondering where he is, too. He is still in the swampy woods, and he hasn't the least idea how to get out of them. The sun is still under a cloud. He doesn't know what time it is, nor which way is North, or, for that matter, South, East, or West.

"If I only had a compass!" he murmurs, and then, "If I only had some cake and a cup of cocoa!"

22

Cousin Clement chases a butterfly, while Caleb waits in the calash.
Caleb wears a coachman's cockade in his hat.

He is extremely hungry. Caterpillar lets himself down on a silk thread, and swings back and forth near some wild cherries until Apple sees them and tries to eat them, but they are too sour. He finds chestnut burrs, but the chipmunk, the one that threw the acorn that surprised him (unless the oak tree threw it), or some of the chipmunk's friends or relations must have eaten the chestnuts months ago.

Apple isn't surprised at that.

But he is surprised to see a chimpanzee looking down from a bough.

And he is surprised (and a little frightened, but don't tell him I told you that, because he is trying hard to be brave) to see a canoe, carried on the back of an Indian, disappearing in the distance. He wonders if

23

Apple is not surprised to see a chipmunk, a chestnut burr, and a Cinnamon fern beside a small cascade, but he is surprised to see a chimpanzee, and to see a canoe being carried in the distance.

24

this is the Indian who shot the arrow, and thinks he had better hide, and he gathers some leafy branches and holds them over his head, and pretends to be a bush.

Something is happening to Caterpillar. He is determined to stay with Apple to protect him from harm, but he is growing strangely sleepy. He longs to spin a silk blanket, roll himself in it, and close his eyes, but he drops to Apple's cap and struggles to keep awake as no caterpillar has ever struggled before.

I'll just close my eyes, he thinks. I won't go to sleep—I'll just—

Apple is thinking, too, pacing up and down with his hands clasped behind his back. And he makes a great decision.

"I'll follow the Indian!" he says aloud.

If he gives back the arrow, perhaps the Indian will give him some supper and show him the way home.

Or perhaps he won't.

So off goes Apple, with Chimpanzee swinging from tree to tree overhead, and Caterpillar, keeping his promise to stay with Apple, clinging to Apple's cap.

The crocodile goes, too, crawling along, not taking his eyes off Apple for an instant.

D

Deep in the stream-bank's rustling reeds
Deerfoot the Redskin hid,
Clad in his buckskin and his beads,
The whispering pines amid.

The Indian Apple followed is Deerfoot the Redskin, although to tell you the truth—and must we not always tell the truth?—his skin is not really red—more the shade of a rather old penny. He paints himself with blue and yellow paint for Sunday, and the paint stays on all week, unless he is caught in the rain, until he takes his bath on Saturday night.

When Apple finds him squatting by his canoe on the bank of the stream where dragonflies are darting, with his dog beside him, Deerfoot is more discouraged than dangerous. He gives a war whoop at the sight of the Paleface (Apple) but his heart isn't in it. He is on his way home from his hunting with not a thing for supper.

First he saw some fine ducks among the rushes, and shot several, with his bow and arrows, of course. But when his dog splashed in and came back with a duck in his mouth, Deerfoot realized that it and all the others were only decoys made of painted wood.

Deerfoot's dog is named Sir Droppit. When he was a puppy he was fond of chewing things, especially beaded moccasins, war bonnets (eagle feathers for best, turkey feathers for every day) and Deerfoot's baby, the papoose Fawnfoot. Fawnfoot didn't mind; he would chew

26

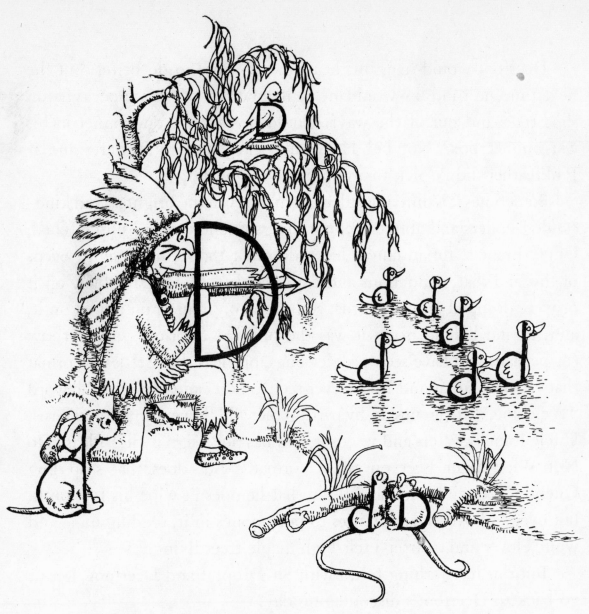

Deerfoot shoots at the ducks, without knowing that they are only decoys. He is watched by his dog, Sir Droppit, the Dove he promised his mother not to shoot, and a Deermouse. A Dormouse was watching, too, but has fallen asleep.

the puppy right back. They both enjoyed it. But Deerfoot and his wife, the Squaw Pinkfeather, shouted "Drop it, sir! Drop it!" so often that the puppy thought that was his name, and would not answer any other.

Deerfoot's old mother said it was Deerfoot's fault that every moccasin and war bonnet in the wigwam was chewed to pieces.

"If I have told you once, I have told you a thousand times to put your things away neatly when you take them off."

Deerfoot would hang his head and promise to do better, but the next time he came in would he remember to put his moccasins on shoe trees and out of the way? Would he put his war bonnet in his war-bonnet box? Not he! He would leave them anywhere, and if Pinkfeather didn't pick them up, Sir Droppit did.

Sometimes it is difficult indeed to make even the brightest and kindest dog understand about keeping things unchewed and unscratched. Uncle Francis, for instance, has a doormat that is his delight. Seeds of this and that, dandelions and daisies and feathery grass, blew on it or were dropped on it by birds, sun shone on it and rain rained on it, and, lo and behold, soon it was the prettiest doormat you ever saw (or perhaps you have seen prettier ones, but it is the prettiest doormat that Uncle Francis and I have ever seen). You can only read the word "Welcome," woven into it, by parting the wild flowers, grass, and ferns. Uncle Francis waters and weeds it, and has put a sign by it, "Please Do Not Wipe Your Feet on the Doormat." But does that stop Pug Quentin? Certainly not! I will say that he doesn't wipe his feet on it, but over and over again he tries to bury bones in it, sending moss and white clover and quarter-inch-high maple trees flying.

But this has nothing to do with Sir Droppit and Deerfoot. Let us go back to Deerfoot's discouraging day.

First the ducks that were only decoys.

Next he tried to catch a deermouse, but it got away. (Please do not confuse a deermouse, who is always lively, with a dormouse, who is always sleepy. It hurts their feelings.)

Then there was a Dove he could easily have shot if he hadn't promised his mother never to shoot a dove. Deerfoot's mother is called Squaw Cooing Dove, because she won first prize for being able to shout loudest of any squaw in the tribe. Deerfoot wishes he could hear her now, calling, "D-e-e-r-FOOT! Supper's READ-y!"

And, worst of all, he has used every arrow.

First on the decoy ducks, then on the deermouse that got away, and the last one was the one Apple found.

Not an arrow in his quiver!

How Cousin Gumbo would laugh! he thinks dejectedly.

So that when Apple approaches, holding out the arrow, he is delighted to have it back, and when Apple asks, "If you please, sir, will you tell me how to get home?" he answers quite pleasantly, "How! How!"

"How! How?" Echo answers from the hill.

How, indeed?

E

"How?" Deerfoot, Echo, Apple cry,
Then quickly change to "Who?"
An elephant is drawing nigh,
Come from a distant zoo.

The questions, "How, how?" and "Who, who?" still trembling in the air remind me of another question, "Where, where?" and of Apple's Aunt Ella, Aunt Bella's twin sister, you remember, who, at this very instant, is asking herself, "Where, where can Appleby be? And where are Cousin Clement, Bella, and Francis?"

You and I know that Cousin Clement vanished into the woods in search of a butterfly, but where he is now no one knows, except, possibly, Cousin Clement. We don't know where forgetful Uncle Francis is, but we do know that he forgot to give Aunt Ella the invitation to come to Aunt Bella's birthday tea, and forgot to give Aunt Bella the invitation to come to Aunt Ella's birthday tea. So that now, while Aunt

Bella mournfully waits for Uncle Francis, Cousin Clement, Apple, and Aunt Ella, Aunt Ella impatiently waits for Uncle Francis, Cousin Clement, Apple, and Aunt Bella.

Aunt Ella seized her egg beater and whirred the whites of the eggs Uncle Francis brought until they rose shining and white as snow. The angel-food cake she made from them waits now on the table, together with an epergne full of every kind of flower and fern from her garden, and a basket of strawberries topped, by mistake, by her strawberry-emery bag.

She is not one to sit still and cry into a teacup. She tries to ease her impatience by rearranging the collection of ear shells on her étagère (or whatnot, or stand having shelves for holding ornaments, if you prefer—it's all the same to me and the dictionary and Aunt Ella).

The exquisite ear shells from the Pacific Ocean were presents from Great-Uncle Thomas. He gave them to Aunt Ella when he gave the conch shells and the corals from the Indian Ocean to Aunt Bella.

But even the colors of the ear shells (and if you want to call them abalone shells, go right ahead; it's the same thing), pink flowing into violet, green flowing into gold, like the changing colors in a soap bubble, do not comfort her.

"Where are they?" she cries again (meaning, of course, not the ear shells but Uncle Francis, Cousin—oh, you must know the list of absent guests by now! It ends with "and Apple").

Perhaps it would surprise her to learn that Apple, too, is wondering where he is. He only knows that he is with an Indian deep in the dark and dangerous woods by a wandering stream.

Deerfoot sits brooding by his canoe. He doesn't want to go home without having captured anything, because he feels too silly.

"That the day should come when I, Deerfoot, the Mighty Hunter, would have to fall back on berries and edible roots for my supper! Ugh! Ugh!"

As he speaks these words, an elephant approaches.

30

Aunt Ella beating eggs with her egg beater. An eggshell is by a basket of strawberries, topped, by mistake, with her strawberry emery bag. She has put her Epergne, full of everything from the garden, on top of the Etagère that holds the ear shells Great-Uncle Thomas brought her. He also brought, from Paris, the etching of the Eiffel Tower. Cousin Clement painted the Emperor butterfly.

How would you feel if you saw an unexpected elephant coming toward you through the woods?

That is exactly how Apple feels.

How Deerfoot feels I can't say. There is no telling from his face, for this week he put on his Sunday warpaint in the shape of a blue frown and a yellow sneer. And, as he often says, he is never one to talk about his deepest feelings.

But, certainly, Elephant would be enough for supper, and plenty left over for meat pie, or sliced cold with a salad of Indian cucumber and Indian turnip. So he lets fly his one arrow.

Of course an arrow wouldn't even tickle Elephant, but he is delighted, for he is a young elephant and a timid one, and coming suddenly on Apple and Deerfoot has frightened him. But he thinks the arrow is a welcoming present, so, in return, he tears up a bouquet of whatever happens to be growing together—ferns, grasses, and a silver birch tree that Deerfoot had his eye on—had both eyes on, in fact—for making a new birch-bark canoe when the tree grew large enough, and presented the lot to Deerfoot. Then Elephant, always longing to make friends, goes through his tricks—waltzing, standing on his head, standing up and saluting with his trunk—and the chimpanzee who surprised Apple and is still watching from the treetop, goes through all *his* tricks, before a spellbound audience of Deerfoot, Deerfoot's dog Sir Droppit, an egret that hurries up from the swampy pond, Crocodile, who has forgotten to pretend to be a log in his interest in wondering how Chimpanzee would taste for dessert after a light supper of Appleby, and Apple himself—and Caterpillar, watching with round eyes that he can hardly force to stay open.

Elephant and Chimpanzee end their performance, trunk in paw, bowing. Apple's cap fell off—Caterpillar just managed to drop from it to Apple's shoulder—and Chimpanzee is wearing it. I fear that Apple will never get it back.

Perhaps you think it is unusual to find an elephant, a chimpanzee, an adjutant bird, usually found in India, and a crocodile (whose snap-

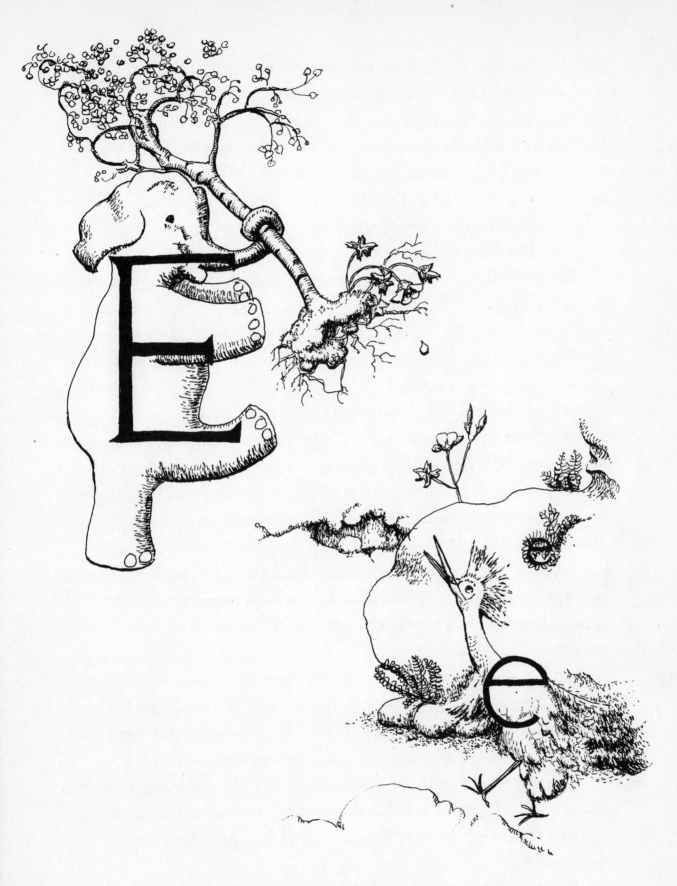

An egret hurries to watch Elephant's exhibition.
The ferns on the rock are called ebony spleenwort.

ping jaws are now filling the air with noises like gun shots) in the woods. You are right. It is most unusual. You might go into those woods every day for a year and not see anything more surprising than a rabbit. But today Mr. Kelly, the keeper of the Zoo, for once was careless, and, after giving Elephant his dinner, a delicious bale of hay, hurried off for his own dinner, his favorite corned beef and cabbage, without making sure that the door of the Elephant House was fastened.

And Elephant walked out.

Before he left the Zoo, he went to each cage and opened each door, for he has a kind heart and believes in sharing his pleasures, so that a great many creatures came with him, crawling, flying, running, or riding on his back, and everyone was happy except Mr. Kelly when he came back from his dinner.

But everyone is happy no longer.

Deerfoot hasn't been happy all afternoon—being fooled by those decoy ducks depressed him dreadfully—and now, picking up his last arrow that didn't get him even an elephant, he and Sir Droppit go off down the stream in his canoe, so swiftly and silently that no one notices, except the egret that flies away.

Elephant suddenly has an attack of shyness and swings off, with Chimpanzee riding on his back, and the whispering pines and the hemlocks whisper as he pushes between them; the green curtains of their branches close after him.

And Apple is left alone.

No, not alone. As he stands there, hungry, frightened, Cousin Clement's birthday present not found, the way home not found, and the shades of evening falling, he stands between friend and foe.

The friend is Caterpillar. Spinning a length of the silk that he is longing to make into a soft blanket to wrap himself in, he fastens it to Apple's collar, lets himself down, and tries to pull Apple away from the crocodile.

But Apple stands as though he were spellbound, gazing into those snapping jaws, and does not even feel Caterpillar's tiny tugging.

34

Caterpillar wearily creeps up Apple again and onto his shoulder.

I'm not the climber I used to be, he thinks. These high places make me dizzy.

But he dares not rest. If Apple is eaten, Caterpillar will be eaten, too, for he will never desert this friend in danger. He humps himself into an arch, with every bristle down his back bristling, trying to frighten Crocodile.

The foe, as you have guessed before now, is Crocodile, who, with one more snap of his jaws that rolls through the woods like thunder, begins to crawl closer and closer.

F

Now Uncle Francis thought that he
Would to the water hie.
He said, "It's useless, you can see,
To fish where it is dry."

Meanwhile Common Silverside (and please don't tell me you have forgotten her, the little fish who set out to save Apple from Crocodile) is swimming too fast down the stream to flip a fin or blow a bubble at the schools of friends and relatives that hail her.

"What's got into Cousin Common?" they ask each other, swinging in her backwash and goggling after her.

When Crocodile claps his jaws, she thinks it is thunder, and anxiously puts her head out of the water to see whether a storm is coming to drive away her friend who will help Apple. But there are no raindrops

35

on the roof of the stream, the sky is cloudless blue, the deepening blue that tells of coming evening, a frog she knows sits peacefully among forget-me-nots that look down at the water with their blue eyes, and there, among unfurling fern fronds, are the feet of her friend.

Let me tell you something that may or may not surprise you. Follow the feet upward, and at the top you will find the face of Uncle Francis.

After he took the eggs and the invitation from Aunt Bella to Aunt Ella, and forgot to leave the invitation, and brought back another invitation from Aunt Ella to Aunt Bella (both invitations are in his pocket at this very minute), he went into his kitchen (Aunt Bella's kitchen, too, of course, and Pussy's and Quentin the pug's kitchen) to leave the egg basket that was now a strawberry basket, and there on the table were some extra delicacies for the birthday party that Uncle Francis had forgotten.

Did these preparations remind him of it?

Not at all!

He emptied the strawberries into a bowl, hardly eating any as he did it—not more than two dozen, and leaving the most enormous ones for Aunt Bella—then filled the basket with food, figs, fresh fruits, and a frosted cake, picked up his fishing rod, and was off to the stream.

Uncle Francis is fond of nature, of fish and flowers and birds that fly, of all the creatures that wear fur or feathers. And the fish are fond of Uncle Francis, as he never uses a hook but just ties something good to the end of his line and lets them eat it off.

"Let others enjoy themselves fencing with their foils or dancing the fandango with their castanets and their fans around the fountains of old Madrid, but give me fishing," Uncle Francis always says.

Common Silverside is one of his great friends, and now he ties a bit of frosted cake to his line and lets it down to her.

Instead of eating it, she tugs at the line, trying to lead Uncle Francis to where Apple is in danger.

She tugs so hard, poor tired little fish, that her kind friend follows

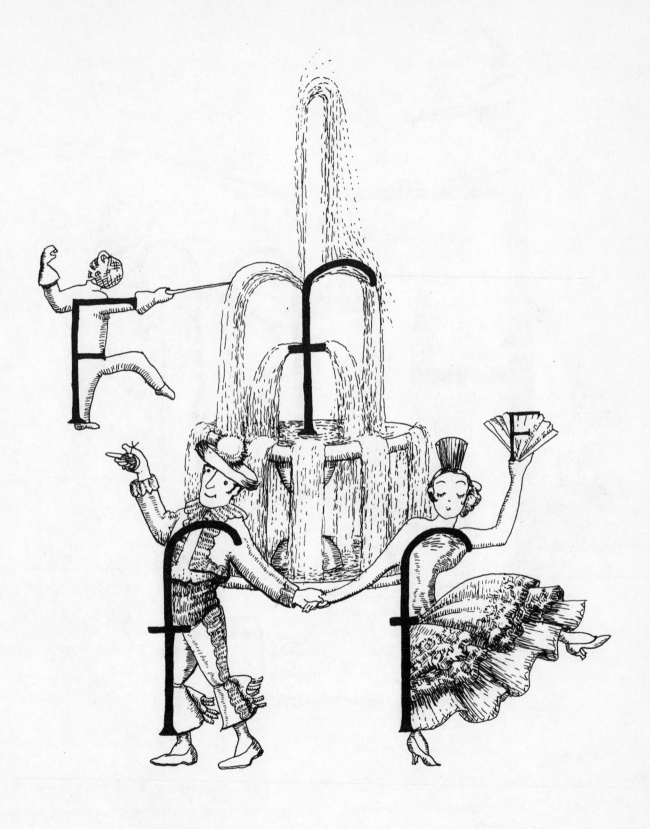

The Spanish lady with her Fan, and the gentleman, dance a fan-dango in front of a fountain, while a Fencer fences with his foil.

Uncle Francis fishing. He has put a feather in his hat, and is having so much fun that he has not noticed the flamingos among the flowering flags, or the frog near the forget-me-nots, or the fern-fronds unfurling. He is feeding the fish with fragments of frosted cake from his basket. The butterfly over the fresh fruit (a freestone peach) is called a Fritillary. No Zebra butterfly here.

along the bank, laughing so merrily at the idea of a fish catching a man that he doesn't even notice two bright pink flamingos watching with interest. They are friends of Elephant's, of course.

Will Uncle Francis and Common Silverside reach Apple in time to save him from Crocodile?

And what will become of the basket, still full of fruit, figs, filberts, and other dainties as well as a few forget-me-nots that forgetful Uncle Francis has gathered to take to Aunt Bella?

G

Let us go on a moment, please,
To where, beside his wigwam roomy
Beneath the whispering forest trees,
Glum Gumbo crouches, looking gloomy.

Now where are we?

You and I are with Gumbo, Deerfoot's cousin, in front of his wigwam. Where are all the others?

Aunt Bella is feeling more and more anxious. Cockatoo and Pussy cat and Bob, her birdie dear, are asleep, and while Quentin the pug is nowhere to be seen, he always turns up for his supper. She isn't anxious about them. She is anxious about her other loved ones. She stands at the window looking out for them.

A goldfinch on a globe of thistledown sings an evening song, then tucks its head under its wing and goes to sleep.

39

A guinea hen walks past the window and vanishes into the meadow where she has hidden her nest.

But there is no sign of Uncle Francis, Aunt Ella, Cousin Clement, or Apple on their way to her party.

Aunt Ella is standing at her window, too, and is feeling more and more impatient. All she sees is Nanny, the goat that belongs to Uncle Francis and Aunt Bella, standing on the roof of the summer house. Aunt Ella isn't going to put up with that for a minute. Out she rushes (she is very quick and light on her feet, and when she and Aunt Bella and Cousin Kate—you haven't met Cousin Kate yet, but you will meet her—were girls, they were so nimble that people called them the Three Graces).

"Shoo! Shoo!" cries Aunt Ella, throwing a greening apple, which Nanny goat eats with a bow and a smile.

When Aunt Bella, Aunt Ella and Cousin Kate were girls, people called them the Three Graces. Here they are dancing The Dance of the Butterflies. They had gauze wings sewn on their green gowns, and wreaths of golden-yellow roses on their heads. "Weren't we gay?" says Aunt Bella. "Weren't we graceful?" says Cousin Kate. "Weren't we geese?" says Aunt Ella.

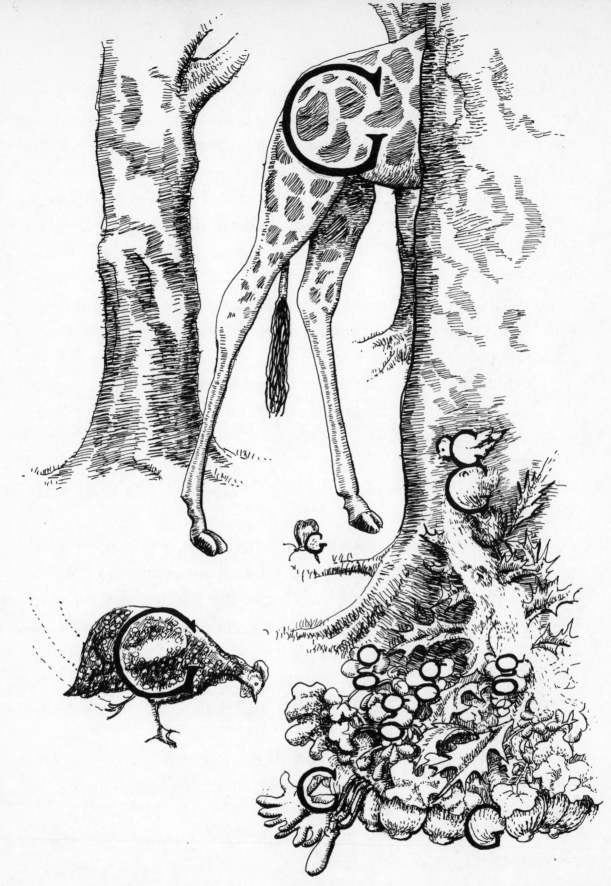

From her window Aunt Bella sees a Guinea Fowl, and a Goldfinch on a globe of thistledown. The thistle is growing in a bed of geraniums, edged with shells called Great Cockles, brought from Africa by Great-Uncle Thomas. The goldfinch sees a butterfly—oh, no, not a Zebra, a Glass-Wing—the Glass-Wing sees the Guinea Fowl scratching gravel, the Guinea Fowl sees a pair of Gardening-gloves. No one sees a Giraffe going gently by.

Uncle Francis is still running along the stream bank, led by Common Silverside, except when he thinks it is his turn to do the leading, and runs in the opposite direction, pulling the desperate little fish the wrong way.

Caleb the coachman, crouched on the seat of the calash by the edge of the woods, hears a crackling in the underbrush, straightens, gives a flip of the reins to rouse Hotspur, the old horse, and says, "Here comes Mr. Clement."

It is only a giraffe who strolls out of the woods, looks down at Caleb with large, gentle eyes, and ambles down the road. One of Elephant's friends, I needn't tell you.

Caleb doesn't believe for a minute that he has really seen a giraffe.

"Dreaming again," he murmurs. "Wish someone would tell me where Mr. Clement is."

I can't, can you?

But we do know where we are. We are here with Glum Gumbo in front of his wigwam.

You and I like to toast marshmallows over a fire, but Gumbo prefers toasted gopher, even though you and I and the gopher do not. He caught a fine fat gopher, and built a glowing bonfire, and balanced the gopher on the end of his toasting fork, and smacked his lips at the thought of his good supper.

But the gopher, after going through some tricks, pretending to tremble, pretending to wipe away a tear with its paw (just showing off), jumped down and vanished into the forest.

That is why Gumbo is glum and gloomy. Here is his glowing fire, with the tiny fires of the glowworms beginning to shine all around it. But where is anything to cook?

"Wild grapes again," he grumbles, picking a bunch. "Wild grapes yesterday, wild grapes every day!"

Among gentians and wild geraniums, shining with globes of evening dew, some pale yellow Glistening Coprinus have risen. The Glis-

Glowworms glow among the wild grapes and on the grass by the mushrooms called Glistening Coprinus, that have risen among bottle gentians and wild geranium, so that Glum Gumbo knows that it is suppertime, and tries to grill a gopher over the glowing fire.

tening Coprinus is an edible mushroom, in case you have forgotten for the moment. Gumbo gathers them, too.

"Vegetable Plate again!" he groans. "How Cousin Deerfoot would laugh!"

He doesn't know that a short time ago Deerfoot was saying, about his own troubles, "How Cousin Gumbo would laugh!"

Now I think everyone is accounted for; let me see.

Aunt Bella, Bob the birdie, Cockatoo and Pussy the cat, Aunt Ella and Nanny the goat, Uncle Francis and Common Silverside, Caleb and Hotspur the horse, Gumbo and the gopher.

Cousin Clement, Deerfoot, and Sir Droppit the dog are certainly somewhere.

Oh!

I forgot Apple!

H

Homeward the herds are mooing by,
The first pale stars are shining,
And underneath the hemlocks high
A homesick heart is pining.

The homesick heart is not in the bosom of Uncle Francis, who is still romping up and down through the harebells at the edge of the stream, with poor little Common Silverside at the other end of his fishing line. He is getting so out of breath that he fears he may fall flat on his face, but he thinks his friend is enjoying herself so much that he forces himself to keep running.

Hotspur the Horse sees a Herder driving a herd of Holstein cows home between the hedges and the hayfields full of haystacks and harebells, and decides to go home himself. The chipping sparrow on the dashboard is often called a hairbird, because it lines its nest with horsehair. That is why it is looking hopefully at Hotspur's tail.

The homesick heart is not in the bosom of Cousin Clement, wherever he is, for when he is hunting butterflies or moths, he is happy, and when he is not hunting them, he always comes home.

The homesick heart is not in the bosom of Caleb, because, waiting in the calash, he has fallen peacefully asleep, and Hotspur the horse, deciding it is time for supper, is taking him home. First Aunt Bella sees the calash pass, and calls to ask Caleb if Cousin Clement and Apple are inside; then a mile down the road Aunt Ella does the same thing. And, because Caleb's head is nodding up and down in time with Hotspur's jog trot, each lady thinks he is nodding "Yes."

"Oh, what a comfort!" Aunt Bella sighs, smiles at the motto Cousin Lucy embroidered for her that says "Home Sweet Home" (don't try to remember who Cousin Lucy is—you haven't met her yet), murmurs, "How true!" and goes out to sit in her howdah in the fragrant twilight until Uncle Francis returns.

I must tell you about her howdah. Great-Uncle Thomas, coming home from a visit to India, made a howdah sound so comfortable that Aunt Bella wished that she had one, if she could have it without an elephant moving about beneath it.

"Nothing easier!" cried Great-Uncle Thomas, and the next time he came home from one of his voyages he brought her one from the Vale of Kashmir. She has it in the garden, and there she and Uncle Francis spend happy hours, watching the hummingbirds in the honeysuckle, he in his hammock between the horse-chestnut trees and she in her howdah.

You, I'm sure, and Great-Uncle Thomas and I prefer howdahs on the backs of elephants, and Great-Uncle Thomas used to ride in his in India on an elephant who just happened to be the great-uncle of our elephant, the one who waltzed for Apple and Deerfoot in the woods. Isn't it strange that the two great-uncles should know each other, and years later their two great-nephews should know each other?

Aunt Bella is not really worried about Uncle Francis. Like Quentin the pug, sooner or later he is sure to turn up for his supper. She believes

A happy hour for Aunt Bella in her Howdah and Uncle Francis in his Hammock under the Horse-Chestnut trees. Aunt Bella has the Hassock to help her hop in and out of the Howdah. Honeysuckle has climbed over the Howdah, which never happened in the days when it was moving about on the back of an elephant. Hummingbirds are helping themselves to honey from the flowers, and one hummingbird thinks that Uncle Francis is a flower.

47

Cousin Clement and Apple are safe and together, and sooner or later will give some good reason for not coming to her party, such as "We forgot." Now her only worry is why Ella didn't come.

A mile down the road, Aunt Ella is wondering why Bella didn't come.

And at exactly the same instant (6:42 by Aunt Ella's electric clock and 3:02 with twenty-two cuckoo calls by Aunt Bella's cuckoo clock) both sisters cry, "I do believe Francis forgot to give her the invitation!"

Here are Bella and Ella when they were little, giving each other a Happy Hug because of the House for their dolls that Uncle Thomas gave them. He gave them Hero, the Hobbyhorse, too, and the picture of the Hippopotamus. Cousin Clement gave them the picture of a hair-streak hedgerow butterfly and a hyacinth. One of the twins tore the picture of the heron out of a book. I won't tell you which; the only hint I will give is that Bella didn't do it.

48

And they run along the lane toward each other and meet with a happy hug.

That has always been their way. When they were little girls, Great-Uncle Thomas (much younger then, of course, but already giving presents) gave them a doll house, and still tells about how they hugged each other for joy.

"It was a sight for sore eyes!" Great-Uncle Thomas says.

Not that his eyes were sore; they have always been unusually strong, and even now, although he wears spectacles sometimes, they have no glass in them. They are just for fun, to hold on a big red false nose. He only wears them when he thinks someone needs cheering.

But to get back beneath the hemlocks high to that homesick heart.

Deerfoot and Gumbo are beneath the hemlocks high, but Gumbo was at home when we met him, and Deerfoot is probably in his own wigwam by now, so that they aren't homesick.

That leads us to Apple, and high time, too.

When last we saw the brave boy, Crocodile was crawling toward him, and all seemed lost.

But no!

Up the wide stream comes something large and gray, like a submarine with a pleasant smile, and Crocodile sinks until again it looks as harmless as an old log. A heron comes and stands on it, unalarmed.

Apple, with one look at the new arrival (a hippopotamus, a friend of Elephant's from the Zoo, you may be sure), runs so hard that his homesick heart (we have found that homesick heart at last), nearly pounds out of his side, and the bristling spines of Caterpillar, clinging to his shoulder, are blown flat.

I

An ilex tree grows in the wood,
Covered with many a berry.
Can Apple climb it? If he could
He'd feel a lot more merry.

The very instant that Apple and Caterpillar depart at top speed—the branches are still shaking behind them—Uncle Francis and Common Silverside arrive at top speed.

The hippopotamus puts its head under, so that all Uncle Francis sees are an old log and a gray rock in the stream, but Common Silverside sees Crocodile-log's and Hippopotamus-rock's frightening faces through the water, doesn't see Apple, is sure that they have eaten him between them, and thinks, "All is lost! Too late!"

With one exhausted gasp, she rises and floats on the top of the stream.

Uncle Francis thinks that, in trying to give pleasure to her, he has killed her, and reverently bares his head.

Does he see the tiniest quiver in the small sliver of silver? Or is it the motion of the water?

With a faint stir of hope, he scoops her and as much of the stream as it will hold into his hat, and hurries home by a short cut, forgetting his basket.

Meanwhile Apple with Caterpillar crouched on his shoulder like a jockey on a race horse, has run himself dizzy, and sinks gasping against a tree.

He springs back, with a feeling that he has fallen into a mixture of a beehive, Cousin Lucy's needle book, and the claws of Pussy the cat, for the tree is an ilex tree, and that is another name for holly, and you know how holly leaves can prick you.

Now that the blood has stopped roaring in his ears, he hears another sound—something enormous coming through the woods, closer, closer—

Prickles or no prickles, he must climb the tree, and he tries.

Out from the trees comes Elephant, with Chimpanzee riding grandly on his back, still wearing Apple's cap and fanning himself with a green bough.

Elephant's ivory tusks gleam through the gloaming, and remind us that we have elephants to thank, if we like playing on the piano, or blame, if we don't enjoy practicing scales, for the ivory of piano keys.

Apple's Cousin Kate plays very nicely, and often says, "Apple, if you would only practice, you could play the piano nicely, too."

But Apple would rather play games.

Once in the twilight, while the grown-ups sat on the porch, he rolled two oranges gently back and forth over the ivory keys. They all thought he was playing with his ten fingers.

"Sweet!" whispered Aunt Bella.

"Like water murmuring around a fishing boat," said Uncle Francis.

"Just a song at twilight," sighed Cousin Lucy.

"How Appleby has improved! Quite a touch!" said Cousin Kate. "I know that piece—what is its name? It's just at the tip of my tongue—

But remembering all this isn't helping Apple now.

Elephant realizes by Apple's troubled face and frantic efforts and cries of "Ouch!" that he wants to get into the top of the tree.

Nothing easier!

Elephant wraps his trunk around the smooth trunk of the ilex and pulls it up by the roots, laying the top of it at Apple's feet.

51

We know about the Ilex tree, the Ibis among the Swamp Iris, and the insect-eating plants with insects flying above them. But who is the little Indian boy? Probably we will find out sooner or later.

He is sorry to see that this does not make Apple happy.

He tries again to guess what Apple wants, and lifts him, carefully and s-l-o-w-l-y, and, by accident, upside down. Everything falls out of Apple's pockets—a pencil, a small notebook, half a dog biscuit intended for Quentin the pug, a whistle that has lost its voice, a nutshell, a snail shell, a locust shell, a top shaped and colored like a radish, a decalcomania picture of a clown riding a pig, a silver-looking horseshoe that came out of a Christmas cracker, and, from the same cracker, a snapper that hasn't snapped and a motto that says

If I should offer you a kiss,
Would that offend you, my dear Miss?

Also, a piece of pink string full of knots, some mixed crumbs, a handkerchief that he had used for a paint rag when he was painting butterflies with Cousin Clement, with a piece of butterscotch and a Turkish stamp from a letter from Great-Uncle Thomas stuck to it, and, what Apple prizes most of all his possessions, a stone that sparkles like diamonds—

Where have we got to?

Oh, yes! Elephant is still s-l-o-w-l-y lifting Apple, and now puts him high in another tree, bows, and modestly withdraws, not wanting to be thanked.

Chimpanzee eats the butterscotch and the Turkish stamp, and, waving the handkerchief, swings through the treetops after Elephant, leaving the other things scattered among the clumps of gleaming white Indian pipes that have pushed up through the moss, and leaving Apple in the treetop, alone with a few early stars and Caterpillar.

An inchworm rises from a leaf, to Caterpillar's joy. At last someone who speaks his language!

He pours out his tale of danger and daring, or tries to, for Inchworm, who has never moved far from his birthplace, isn't much interested.

"Let others travel," he says. "Home is good enough for me."

53

"Have you ever seen a log that crawled toward you and opened its mouth until it was as big as a cave, and shut it and made thunder come?"

"Let—me—think," says Inchworm. "Maybe I have and maybe I haven't."

"Have you ever seen a huge gray rock swim toward you with a terrible smile on its face?"

"No, and I wouldn't care to; give me peace and quiet. No dangers at all, here at home."

No dangers? Even as Inchworm speaks, an ichneumon fly, the mortal enemy of worm and caterpillar, hovers near on the evening air. Just below, in a wet patch of the woods where blue petals of wild iris have almost vanished in the blue of twilight, grow insect-eating plants, with green and crimson leaves shaped like pitchers and full of honeydew to tempt thirsty, hungry insects. Let any insect go in for a drink, and SNAP! Down comes a lid of leaf, the cup is a trap, and that is the end of the insect, and a good meal for the plant. No dangers, when at the top of the tree several indigo buntings are talking in drowsy bird talk about having supper, just a bite of worm, perhaps, before they go to sleep? No dangers, indeed!

"No dangers here," says Inchworm, and begins to show off, humping, then stretching from the branch as straight as a tiny twig. "Can you do this?"

"Anyone can hump," says Caterpillar. "Have you ever seen a huge gray rock—?"

"Often, often. Anyone can hump, but let me see you do this!" Inchworm stretches straight up, then leans from side to side.

"A huge gray rock that pulls up trees, and then dances?"

"You really ought to try it for the good of your figure. Do what I'm doing, I mean, not pull up trees and dance. Although I find dancing excellent exercise, and graceful, too." Inchworm sways gracefully. "Excuse me for mentioning it, but you are too fat."

"I'm not fat. It's my fur coat," says Caterpillar, and curls himself

Inchworm is having a swing from a thread he has spun, and thinking "No danger here!" He does not notice his enemy, the Ichneumon Fly. He does not notice the Indigo Buntings above him, talking about where to go for a bite of worm for supper. Luckily for him, none of them notice him, either.

into a ball, while Inchworm inches off along the branch, each of them thinking about the other, "He talks too much!"

Apple has not noticed either of them. Swaying gently, feeling safe, seeing the stream winding back to the swamp, and no sign of Crocodile, nothing but a white cloud moving slowly over the swamp iris, he ought to be happy.

But he isn't, quite. His homesick heart has stopped thumping, but it is still homesick.

What he thinks is a white cloud is another of Elephant's friends from the Zoo, a wading bird called an ibis. Its white-feathered body shows through the dusk, but not its black tail and long black legs and long black neck and long black beak.

At home in Egypt, on the River Nile, the ibis likes to eat crocodile eggs. Perhaps it is looking for them now. But here it is more likely to find Crocodile himself, and a whole crocodile wouldn't be of the least use to an ibis.

Apple stretches a foot to see if he can reach a lower branch.

He can't.

He has always wished that he might stay up as late as he liked, but now he feels that he is going to stay much, much more up, much, much later than he likes.

One of the indigo buntings flies into his face and backs off in the air with an indignant "Cheep!" Apple is so startled that he nearly falls out of the tree. But that's no good way to get down.

If enough birds came and took my clothes in their bills, they could carry me down, he thinks. He imagines it clearly. He tries to sing like a bird to attract them to him. After the indignant indigo bunting, no other birds come, but Apple, so sleepy that he is half dreaming, goes flying, down, up, home, wherever he wants to go. It is so real in his imagination that he puts his hand over his shoulder to feel a wing, and, instead, touches Caterpillar's small furry body.

That makes him feel less lonely for a moment.

"Hello! A caterpillar!" he says. "Don't worry, I'll get you down somehow."

Caterpillar does not speak or understand English, of course. But the rumble of Apple's voice feels friendly, and he says in his own language, in a voice so small that as far as I know only other caterpillars, moths, butterflies, and so on can hear it, "You see you needn't have worried. I've got you through safely."

Aunt Bella often says of Quentin the pug, Aunt Ella often says of Nanny the goat, Uncle Francis often says of Common Silverside, Caleb often says of Hotspur the horse, Cousin Kate often says of her kitten, Deerfoot often says of Sir Droppit the dog, Mr. Kelly the keeper often says of Elephant:

"That—"

   (*pug, goat, fish, horse, kitten, dog, elephant*)

"understands every word I say."

And Quentin, Nanny, Common Silverside, Hotspur, Kitty, Sir Droppit, and Elephant say in return:

"That—"

   (*lady, woman—Nanny the goat isn't as polite as Quentin the pug, but then, people aren't as polite to her as they are to Quentin; no one has ever thrown greening apples at Quentin, shouting, "Shoo! Scat! Get off that roof!"—perhaps because Quentin wouldn't think of getting on a roof. Whatever the reason, he always says lady while Nanny always says woman. Please excuse me for interrupting myself; I'd better start at the beginning again.*)

"That—"

(*lady, woman, gentleman, gentleman, lady, Indian brave, gentleman*)

"understands every word I say."

Now Apple and Caterpillar, looking at each other with trustful eyes, say together:

"That—"

"understands every word I say."

Far off, below, Apple see something the size and color of an orange marigold glowing in the dusk. It is Gumbo's big bonfire, where the hungry Indian is now gloomily trying a little of this and a little of that in a pot where he is boiling the Glistening Coprinus (those mushrooms, you know)—first a few grapes, then a few blackberries, some Indian turnips, some slivers of slippery elm.

"It needs just a pinch of *something*," he sighs.

Apple is sighing, too. The trunk of the tree is too big to hold and slide down, the lower branches are too far below to reach, too slender to jump on. Apple thinks that he must choose between starving to death in the treetop or falling and breaking every bone.

All alone, he thinks.

We know that he is not alone. His loyal friend Caterpillar is with him, feeling that at last Apple is safe. Where can one be safer than in a treetop? Safe, and surrounded by good things to eat, Caterpillar thinks, nibbling a leaf, too sleepy to want much supper. Then he anchors himself to Apple's collar with the silk thread he spins out of himself, shrugs and wriggles out of his fur coat, spins his cocoon, and goes to sleep.

J

Now what is climbing up the tree?
No wonder that you ask it!
Jocko, a monkey roaming free,
Bearing a well-filled basket.

Jocko usually is minding his own business. Besides his red cap and red jacket he owns a hand organ that plays three tunes—"O Sole Mio," "The Wearing of the Green," and something else that no one has ever been able to remember the name of—and an Italian gentleman, a Signor (Italian for Mister) Olivetto, to turn its handle and do the heavy work of carrying the pennies Jocko collects in his cap.

But sometimes a monkey gets tired of being chained to his business, and Jocko is giving himself and Signor Olivetto a holiday.

On his arm is a basket holding food—figs, fresh fruit, and frosted cakes. There are also a few faded forget-me-nots.

Yes, you are right. It is Aunt Bella's egg basket that Uncle Francis forgot when he went scampering along the stream with Common Silverside.

Jocko pauses at the foot of the tree to put Apple's spilled belongings in the basket, all except the dog biscuit that he eats and the crumbs that the indigo buntings ate long ago and the pink string that a lady indigo bunting took to weave into a nest. He also eats a jam sandwich and part of a jumble from the basket, on the way up the tree.

Jocko likes jumbles, but he likes peanuts better. Elephant also

Jocko.

likes peanuts, but his favorite food is watermelon, rind and all. Gumbo the Indian thinks he would like toasted gopher, as you know. Deerfoot pretends that he only cares for buffalo meat, because he thinks that sounds right for an Indian, but he has never even seen a buffalo, and really his favorite dish is corn pudding. Aunt Bella's birdie Bob loves a lettuce leaf, while Aunt Bella herself thinks nothing in the world is as good as really good pound cake. She says that one of her happiest memories of childhood is of her mother making pound cake and letting her take her forefinger and scrape out the sugary yellow batter that was left in the mixing bowl, which she would then pop into her mouth —her finger, of course, not the bowl. Let me see, what were we talking about? Oh, yes! Aunt Ella likes potato and gravy. Uncle Francis likes cherry pie. Common Silverside's choice would always be a breadcrumb, and Caterpillar likes fresh leaves. Apple likes chocolate ice cream best. Crocodile thinks he is going to like Appleby better than anything he has ever eaten, and can hardly wait to taste him.

Apple has forgotten Crocodile for the moment, but if you were in the treetop and looked down at the rushes in the swamp, you could see them moving now as though something large and long was slowly crawling through them. Crocodile hasn't forgotten Apple.

Oh, excuse me! I meant to ask, What do you like best to eat?

Apple doesn't see the motion in the rushes, for his eyes are on Jocko, who has popped through the leaves like a jack-in-the-box, in his scarlet cap and jacket, with jumble crumbs and jam all over his face. Nor does Apple see the jaguar (another holiday-maker let out of his cage by Elephant) that has startled Jocko into scrambling up the tree.

After they have shaken hands, Apple and Jocko eat the contents of the basket, except for some of the spilled treasures, such as the whistle that won't whistle, the top, and so on, that Apple puts back in his pockets, and the motto from the Christmas cracker, that flutters to earth.

The forget-me-nots Apple puts in his buttonhole, to remind him not to forget:

1. To return, somehow, to his dear friends and relatives.
2. To find the butterfly named the Zebra, in order to give Cousin Clement a look at it for a birthday present, although it seems probable now that his birthday will be over before he and Apple meet again.
3. To remember something else that, just for the moment, he can't recall.

Several June bugs try to share the feast, and a jackdaw makes off with the silver-looking horseshoe, but neither Apple nor Jocko would have cared to eat that.

Little does Apple think that his own dear Aunt Bella made these frosted cakes, or that these fresh figs grew in the conservatory of his own dear Cousin Clement.

Strengthened by his supper and reminded by the forget-me-nots, our hero again tries to think how to get home.

If Elephant came back, he thinks, and lifted me down, it would be easy. Jocko and I could ride him home.

Great-Uncle Thomas, as you know, was fond of riding elephants. You have heard of him in his howdah riding Jumbo—although I don't think I told you that our Elephant's great-uncle in India is named Jumbo.

Jumbo was lent to Great-Uncle Thomas by a friend of his, a prince, the Maharaja of Some-Place-or-Other, I've forgotten just where, and was always decorated grandly, by the Maharaja's orders, before Great-Uncle Thomas rode him. Jumbo's toenails were gilded, his tusks were painted vermilion, with bands of gold, and his trunk and cheeks and ears and sides were painted with enormous flowers, all colors. A gold net, knotted and fringed with pearls, and with long pearl tassels on each side, hung on his forehead. His longest blanket was grasshopper-green, over that a shorter one of orange, and then the one under the howdah, of the pinkest pink you ever saw, trimmed with a thousand tiny looking glasses that blazed in the sunlight in a pattern like Common Silverside's scales.

I wonder how Common Silverside is by now.

Jumbo was repainted every day, and you should have seen the color of the river while he was being given his daily bath! He loved taking baths—all elephants do. First his blankets, head net, howdah, various necklaces, collars and bells I haven't mentioned, and Great-Uncle Thomas would be removed. Then Jumbo would go into the river and slowly, slowly sink, to lie on one side while his mahout—that's the man who takes care of an elephant and drives him and usually is his best friend—scrubbed him with a big scrubbing brush, and pink, scarlet, yellow, green, and blue paint streamed off into the water. Then Jumbo would roll over, slowly, slowly, making quite a big wave, to have his other side scrubbed. Often he would give his mahout and himself a shower bath from his trunk, and always, when he came out, he would powder himself with trunkfuls of dust.

Jumbo loves his mahout better than anyone else, but he is very fond of Great-Uncle Thomas, and Great-Uncle Thomas is very fond of him.

Great-Uncle Thomas was also fond of riding around India in a jampan. That is a chair on bamboo poles that rest on the shoulders of four men called jampanees. Great-Uncle Thomas's jampanees were named Jim, Jam, Janjira, and James Jackson, an unusual name indeed for a native of India. Jim and Jam were splendid jampanees, always cheerful, never tired. Janjira was never cheerful and always tired, or so he said, hanging his head until his turban rested on his nose, losing his slippers, and hinting to be allowed to ride in the jampan himself. Great-Uncle Thomas paid no attention to that, you may be sure. James Jackson was full of kind ideas, garlanding the jampan with fresh jasmine, and always carrying a jar of cool water on his head in case Great-Uncle Thomas grew thirsty.

If Apple had Jumbo, or Jumbo's great-nephew Elephant, to lift him down, and a jampan and four jampanees to carry him home, his troubles would be over.

But he hasn't.

From among the rushes Crocodile rears his head, looks straight at Apple, and snaps his jaws.

Our hero trembles so that the leaves sound as though the wind was in them. Now he must do something.

He does.

In India Great-Uncle Thomas sometimes rides Jumbo the elephant, and sometimes rides in a Jampan carried by four Jampanees. Here he is in his Jampan, but you can see Jumbo passing, just in his old everyday blankets, since Great-Uncle Thomas isn't riding him. The two Jampanees whose faces are hidden are Jim and Jam, and you guess which is Janjira, who is never cheerful and always tired, and which is James Jackson, who garlands the Jampan with jasmine and carries a jar of water.

64

Taking his pencil and notebook, he writes:

Dear Everybody,

I take my pencil in hand to tell you that I am lost up a tree and am surrounded by a Crocodile who snaps his jaws at me. If it is not too much trouble, would you kindly rescue me? I am very much upset. Hoping you are the same, I am your loving

Apple

He gives the note to Jocko, hoping that something will come of it.

Before leaving, Jocko dances a jig, then holds out his little red cap to Apple, who, full of gratitude and hope, puts into it his greatest treasure, the stone that sparkles like diamonds.

K

"Oh, please come soon!" our hero sighs.
"It's growing very late—"
And then he hears some piercing cries,
And answers, "Cousin Kate!"

Apple's Cousin Kate is fond of singing, and has so carrying a voice that once, hearing a locomotive whistle, her sister, Apple's Cousin Lucy, called, "Yes, Kate!" and came in from the garden for lunch, and found it was only ten o'clock. But most of the time any piercing sound is Cousin Kate singing.

She is in the habit of singing at odd moments, and Apple thinks this is the oddest of all.

But he is mistaken. What he thinks is Cousin Kate singing is really a kingfisher by the water, telling a lady kingfisher that he loves her.

The kingfisher likes to fish, and his presence always makes Common Silverside nervous.

I wonder how Common Silverside is?

Although she is too far from him for Apple to hear her, Cousin Kate is singing now, you may be sure.

" 'Sweet and low,' " she sings, " 'SWEET AND LOW!' " making the windows rattle, making her kitten purr like a boiling kettle. Cousin Kate is so carried away by her music that she doesn't notice an astonished kangaroo with her baby in her pouch look in at the window and then leap away, nor a koala with her baby on her head, climbing a tree in alarm.

The koala can carry her baby in her pouch, too, but I don't think the kangaroo can carry her baby on her head. Please correct me if I am wrong.

Kangaroo and Koala are part of the expedition from the Zoo made possible by Elephant. The animals have scattered far and wide, excited and delighted by their new experiences, in spite of a few scares, and not one of them is giving a thought to Mr. Kelly, their kind keeper.

Mr. Kelly, you may be sure, is giving many a thought to them, three of his thoughts being:

1. How in the world did they get out?
2. Where in the world are they?
3. How in the world can I get them back?

Cousin Kate might have been surprised if she had noticed the kangaroo and the koala, or she might not. She has often remarked, when she has come on Nanny the goat in odd places, such as the kitchen sink or the bedroom bed, "Nothing can surprise me any more!"

You might or you might not be surprised if you, instead of the kangaroo, had looked in the window, to see that Cousin Kate has blue hair. If you had looked in yesterday, she would have had pink hair. If you look in tomorrow, who knows what you may see?

Cousin Kate has put on her kimono and her knitting-wool wig with the knitting needles still in it, and is singing. Her kitten listens kindly, a Kingfisher tries to make more noise than Cousin Kate, and a Kangaroo and a Koala and their babies think someone is being killed. A butterfly has flown in at the open window toward the Killarney rose under a picture of Apple in kilts. I thought for a moment it was a Zebra butterfly, but it is a Kricogonia.

Kind Mr. Kelly, the Keeper of the Zoo, sees with surprise that the animals are gone, and he is alone except for two kinglets hopping about and a katydid on top of the grass he has brought for Elephant.

68

Cousin Kate's own hair is red, and she always hated it, from the time when she was a child and the other children called her Carrot-Top.

Last Easter Eve she was dyeing Easter eggs, and had some dye left in the seven jelly glasses on the kitchen table. And she thought that dipping locks of her hair in each of the colors—red, pink, yellow, orange (no, she would skip the orange, her hair was orange enough already), yellow, green, blue, violet—would make a pretty change from carrot-color. She expected to look as though she was wearing the rainbow on her head.

It was a disappointment to have her hair come out in mixed shades of dirty green-brown and dirty brown-green, like dead seaweed.

Yet she kept thinking about rainbow hair, and talked of trying stronger Easter-egg dyes.

Almost everyone except Apple urged her not to do anything of the sort. Apple thought it would be fun if they both did it.

Mr. Roberts, a friend of the family, who was fond of giving advice (he was one of the many who advised Cousin Clement and Apple not to put their paintbrushes in their mouths) said, "I wouldn't do it if I were you."

Cousin Kate opened her mouth to say, "I *couldn't* do it if I were you," because Mr. Roberts hasn't a hair on his shining pink head. Then she thought, just in time, how unkind that would be, and, since her mouth was open and she couldn't think of anything both kind and true that she cared to say at the moment, she sang.

She sang, all by herself, the Sextet from an opera called *Lucia*, that usually takes six people. Cousin Kate often says, "If you want a thing well done, do it yourself."

Mr. Roberts clapped so hard and bowed so low that they parted good friends. He takes credit (in a modest way) for keeping her head out of any more Easter-egg dyes.

But the credit really belongs to Cousin Clement.

Cousin Clement usually believes in minding his own business, but he did urge her not to dye her hair.

"It is such a beautiful color," he said.

"Red. Not even scarlet or crimson or—"

"Coral—"

"Or ruby or—"

"Magenta—"

"Or rose-red. Just carrot. I hate it!"

"It is like marigolds."

"Like carrots."

"Like orange marmalade."

"Like carrots."

"Like a bright new penny."

"Like carrots."

"Like a Colias Elis."

"Like car— What's that?"

"An exquisite orange butterfly."

"Oh!" said Cousin Kate, and stopped looking stubborn and cross, for if Cousin Clement thought her hair was like a butterfly, she knew he must think it was beautiful indeed.

Still, she did long to try just a touch of rainbow on her head.

Then Aunt Bella made her a wig; red, orange (she knew Cousin Kate was tired of orange, but she put in just a strand or two, so that it would be like a real rainbow), yellow, green, blue, and violet knitting wool, with a few glass beads for raindrops.

Cousin Kate liked it so much that she made herself a lot of wool wigs, some fancy, like the pale green one for May Day, with a May basket full of pink-and-white tissue-paper apple blossom and a bird's nest woven in it, or the deep purple one full of stars from the Christmas tree, some simple, like the one she is wearing today.

She doesn't wear wigs all the time—not on the days she is able to believe that her hair looks like marigolds, marmalade, a new penny, or an orange butterfly. But there are days when it looks plain carrot to her; it did this morning. And, as she felt like singing lullabies (you remember

70

it was "Sweet and Low" that was rattling the windows), she put on her quietest, simplest blue wig.

It is the same shade as that blue Chinaman on Aunt Bella's teapot, the teapot full of steaming hot tea for the birthday party, that is now cold. For Aunt Bella is still resting in her howdah, smelling honey-suckle, heliotrope, and Heinrich Munch (that's the name of a big pink rose) that all grow more fragrant with evening and dew, humming "Home, Sweet Home" to herself, and forgetting household tasks, such as emptying the teapot.

Let us return to Cousin Kate.

Wait a minute! What is this odd little figure in a scarlet coat and a scarlet cap that has suddenly appeared beside the howdah, offering a folded paper to Aunt Bella?

It is good little Jocko.

Surely now Apple will be rescued!

Aunt Bella is delighted to see Jocko. But she thinks all he wants is a penny, and explains to him that her penny is in her purse in her bureau drawer in her bedroom. She kindly climbs out of the howdah—quite a task, as Aunt Bella is plump and the sides of the howdah are high—and, hand in paw, they go to the house.

Jocko offers her Apple's note again, but it does not enter her head that he wants her to take it. When she leaves him outside while she goes for her penny, he stuffs the note into his pocket, where he keeps the stone that sparkles like diamonds. Then he leaps to the sill of an open window.

Jocko doesn't know that we must not take things belonging to others. He thinks that everything belongs to everyone; a brook does belong to anyone who is thirsty, a wild grape vine does belong to anyone who is hungry, and, as far as Jocko knows, the beautiful white feathers that he sees belong to anyone who wants a beautiful white feather.

He wants one, and he takes one. He has to tug so hard that he falls flat on his back.

71

Cockatoo lets out such a screech that Aunt Bella, with her penny in her hand, almost falls downstairs.

She looks everywhere, but Jocko is gone, and one of Cockatoo's tail feathers is gone, too.

Let us also be gone. Let us go back to Cousin Kate.

We were talking about her wigs, weren't we?

She made Apple a beard, all colors, from left-over ends of wig wool. He values it highly, and, though the ends sometimes get in his mouth, he often wears it when he and Cousin Kate sing duets.

At the moment, of course, Cousin Kate is singing solos. And, at the moment, she has an audience. For a moment only, a small, anxious face topped with a scarlet cap looks in at the window, a long brown paw offers a note—yes, Apple's note.

Then a high trill of Cousin Kate's song sails forth, and the window is empty.

Cousin Kate tosses her arms up, and sings:

"*Adio, mia spinachi bombazina! Cara fromagio tomato blotto! Tra la la la la la la la la la la la la la la la la la la—!*"

Just go on for a hundred *las*, and be sure not to use your fingers for counting. If you lose track, begin again.

Who knows what opera that is from?

The kitten arches his back, his way of bowing, and, flushed with triumph, Cousin Kate whisks into the kimono Great-Uncle Thomas brought her from Japan, and sings straight through *Madame Butterfly*, an opera about a Japanese lady called Madame Butterfly.

You know by now how Great-Uncle Thomas delights in giving presents. He brought Apple a Highlander's costume, kilt, plaid, sporran, bonnet, bagpipes, and all, from Scotland, and often when Cousin Kate sings Scottish ballads, Apple accompanies her on his bagpipes. You should hear them singing and playing "Scots Wha Ha' "! If you were ever within five miles of them when this was going on, you certainly have heard them.

Speaking of Apple, I wonder what is happening to him by now.

72

L

Now Apple hears a sound like thunder
From what a sailor calls the offing
(That means, far off). Says he, "I wonder!
Can that be Cousin Lucy coughing?"

However, he is mistaken. All of us make mistakes sometimes. Cousin Lucy, Cousin Kate's sister, is miles away, in the garden of the house where Cousin Kate is singing.

Cousin Lucy likes to sing, too. She sings love songs and lullabies in a low voice, while she plays her lute.

Once the sisters tried to sing a duet.

" 'Soft o'er the fountain—' "

"Sing, Lucy, sing!" cried Cousin Kate, and Cousin Lucy, who had been singing as loud as she could, hadn't enough breath left to gasp, "I *am* singing, Kate!"

She could only open and shut her mouth, like Common Silverside.

She isn't even singing by herself, now, for she was laid low by a cough and a cold, and was in bed for several days, blowing her nose on her lace handkerchief, drinking hot lemonade, and comforted by loving letters from friends saying, "Please get well." That is why Apple thought the cough he heard was hers.

She tried to do everything she was told to do, in order to get well quickly. When Cousin Kate said, "Now, Lucy, eat every single thing

When Cousin Lucy was laid low by a cold, she tried to eat everything on her tray, to get strong. Here she is trying to eat the spoon. There is a Lump of ice in the Lemonade; a lot of loving Letters say "Please get well." The light of the Lamp has lured a lovely light green Luna Moth.

on this tray," she did try, but she couldn't get very far with the napkin, she couldn't get anywhere with the fork and the spoon, and she gave up without even trying the cup and the plate.

Now she is well, but is still resting her voice.

She did not notice the kangaroo or the koala, because, protected from the sun by a large leghorn hat and from the shade by a light lace shawl, she was looking through her lorgnette at a lovely lily, and a lady-bug that lit on it. Nor did she notice a lyrebird walking through the lettuce bed.

Unless you live in Australia or near the Bird House in a Zoo, you don't often meet lyrebirds. I have known people who did not want to meet them, thinking the name was liarbird. Not at all! As far as I know, the lyrebird is perfectly truthful. Its name comes from having a tail shaped like a lyre, an ancient kind of harp. It has sooty-brown feathers and lays purple eggs (the bird, not the musical instrument), is very shy, and likes to be alone.

Perhaps that is why, after a look at Cousin Lucy, this one disappears behind a lilac bush.

I am sorry Cousin Lucy didn't see it, for she is fond of birds. Her pet lovebirds, Lulu and Lochinvar, are her delight, and she always takes lettuce leaves for birdie Bob when she goes to see Aunt Bella.

Now she is lounging lazily in the twilight, half asleep, so that when something pushes gently against her, she thinks it is Cousin Kate's kitten, and murmurs drowsily, "Kitty, Kitty, Kitty—good little Kitty—"

It is indeed a cat, but one of the larger cats, Leo the lion from the Zoo.

If Cousin Lucy opened her eyes she would be surprised.

But she drowses on, dreaming about a lamb, while Leo strolls down the lane toward Aunt Bella's house, swinging his tail.

Now another visitor pauses by Cousin Lucy, and when you hear that he wears a scarlet coat over a heart still going pit-a-pat from the

75

Cousin Lucy, wearing a light Lace shawl, looks through her lorgnette at a ladybug that has lit on her lovely lilies. Lulu and Lochinvar, her lovebirds, perch on her large Leghorn hat, a Lark and some Leaf-wing butterflies fly around her, but a Lyrebird is leaving.

shocks of Cockatoo's screech and of Cousin Kate's high note, and a scarlet cap on top of a head that is wondering what to do next, you will know, without my telling you, that it is Jocko.

He climbs on the arm of Cousin Lucy's chair, gently lifts the brim of her leghorn hat to look at her sleeping face, and says, "oo!" in a tiny, thoughtful squeak.

Then he lifts her lace shawl and sees the lovely lily she has picked.

One pair of paws can't hold everything. Jocko puts Cockatoo's feather and Apple's note on Cousin Lucy and helps himself to the lily and her lace handkerchief.

Do you remember that Apple, far away in a tree in the woods, thought he heard Cousin Lucy cough and sneeze? If you do, let me compliment you on having a wonderful memory. Now the sound comes again.

I'll tell you what it is. It is Elephant giving a TREMENDOUS sob and sniff; he is so frightened that he can't hold it in another minute.

Gumbo by his wigwam and Deerfoot, pulling his canoe out of the stream, put their ears (one ear each) to the ground and seize their tomahawks, and Uncle Francis, carrying Common Silverside in his hat, thinks it is thunder and runs for home. Leo the lion, strolling along the lane, answers with a roar so loud that Aunt Bella, Aunt Ella, and Cousin Kate run up and down stairs shutting windows; Cousin Kate is so excited that her blue wig falls out into the lily-of-the-valley bed, and she doesn't notice. Mother birds spread their wings to protect their nestlings from the rain that doesn't come. And Jocko's heart jumps and races again.

He stuffs the lily and the lace handkerchief inside his jacket—

Oh, Jocko! *Please* leave Apple's note on top of Cousin Lucy!

His paw wavers between the note and Cockatoo's tail feather.

Jocko, *please*! She will wake and find it, and all will be well with Apple.

Alas! He stuffs the note into his pocket, scampers up a tree and

77

away, leaving the feather to rise and fall with Cousin Lucy's breathing, like a white ship on a gentle summer sea.

In the midst of the general alarm, only Cousin Lucy, birdie Bob, Caleb the coachman, and Caterpillar in his cocoon on Apple's shoulder sleep on.

M

Crash bang! CRASH BANG *!! What* can *this be?*
Elephant, nearly crazy;
A tiny mouse he chanced to see
Resting beneath a daisy.

If there is one thing on earth that frightens Elephant (and there is), it is a mouse. I have heard that all elephants are afraid of mice; they are afraid the mice will run up inside their trunks and stop them from breathing.

I have never heard that mice are afraid of elephants.

The meadow mouse that frightens our Elephant is a gentle baby, but not in the least frightened. When Elephant flings up his trunk, trumpets, and thunders away, she only twitches her big pale-gray, pale-pink-lined ears (big for a mouse—not, of course, for an elephant) and looks after him with enormous eyes.

Then a drop of dew rolls from the daisy onto her nose and terrifies her, and she runs as fast as she can to the family mousehole, while more dew rains from daisies and meadowsweet, and moths glimmer overhead.

Elephant is not the only one who is alarmed, for he is making such

A mouse rests under a marguerite, a moth flies in the evening air, and dew falls from the meadow-flowers.

a racket, running and trumpeting, that he frightens a macaw and a marabou stork (two of his party from the Zoo) nearly out of their feathers.

The marabou stork is our old acquaintance that Apple saw in the swamp, whose other name is adjutant bird. You may be glad to hear that he still has the soft down under his tail feathers, and that it is still white.

The pink marabou that trimmed the bed jacket Cousin Lucy wore when she was in bed, and having to take medicine, probably came from under the tails of some of his East Indian cousins, and I hope and expect that they have grown new down by now.

The marabou stork runs one way, the macaw flies another. Screaming at the top of his lungs, feathers streaming, he streams and screams past Cousin Lucy, still dreaming in the garden.

His scream ends her dream, she hurries into the house crying, "Yes, Kate?" and adds, "Oh, I thought I heard you calling me! You were only singing, weren't you?"

This hurts Cousin Kate's feelings, for she, too, has heard Macaw. For a time there is a slight misunderstanding between the sisters, until Cousin Lucy reminds Cousin Kate that Great-Uncle Thomas has often said that in all his years at sea he has never heard one single mermaid sing as loud as Cousin Kate can. And Cousin Kate, although she says she doesn't believe Great-Uncle Thomas ever heard a single mermaid, or saw one, either, can't help being pleased by this compliment, wipes her eyes and blows her nose and smiles, and they kiss and make up.

Another bird is surprised by Elephant; a dark olive-green motmot with a cap of gleaming turquoise-blue feathers, who has been sitting quietly in a maple tree, minding its own business. Most birds (as far as I know) think that they are pretty enough without doing anything to improve their looks, but not the modest motmot. It has two long black tail feathers that it strips with its bill of the feathery part, except that, just at the tips of the quills, it leaves two black feather ornaments. This doesn't hurt, any more than it does when your hair is cut, but it does mean that the motmot takes time and trouble to make itself, and therefore to make the world, more interesting to look at.

Elephant, with the mouse on his mind, doesn't pause to admire the motmot's tail feathers, you may be sure. And I don't know what has happened to the motmot, for it has hidden itself completely while we were talking about it.

Someone else who is startled by Elephant is an old Indian medicine

80

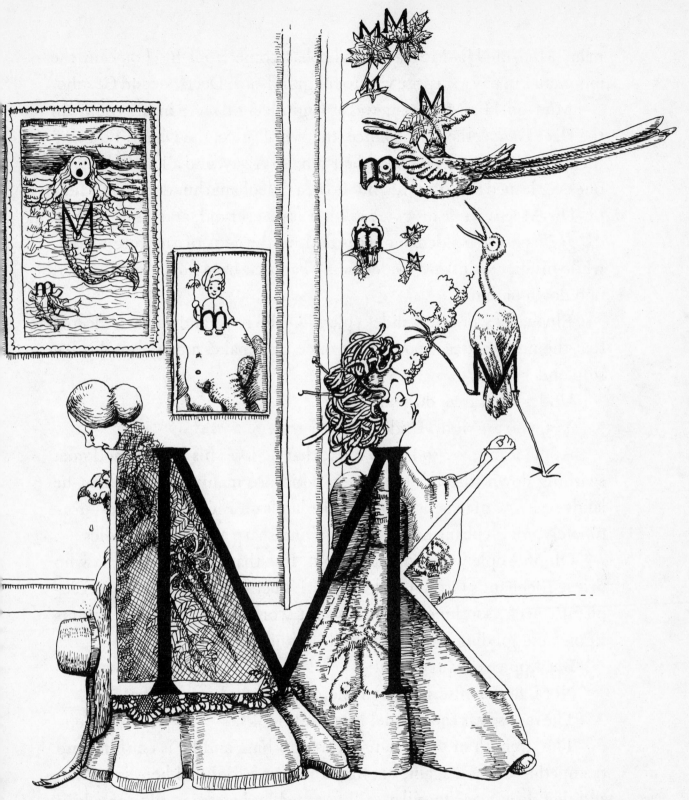

Cousin Lucy thought a macaw screaming was Cousin Kate, Cousin Kate's feelings are hurt, and they are having a Misunderstanding. The macaw is still screaming, scaring a Marabou Stork, but those loving mates, Lulu and Lochinvar, sit quietly on a Maple branch. A mackerel and his mate are in the picture of a Mermaid singing a melody by moonlight. This picture, and the one of a mahout mounted on an elephant, are gifts from Great-Uncle Thomas.

man, Mud-on-His-Moccasins, who has come from his home in the mountains to pay a surprise visit to his grandsons, Deerfoot and Gumbo.

Mud-on-His-Moccasins was a magnificent dancer in his youth. In the Deer Dance, the Corn Dance, the War Dance, the Dance To Bring the Rain, the Dance To Make the Rain Go Away, and all the others, no one ever leaped as high as he. But now, as Elephant thunders past, Mud-on-His-Moccasins leaps twice as high as he ever did, and lands with an "*Ugh!*" on the maidenhair ferns and mushrooms of the forest floor, while his moccasins and his medicine hat, that have flown even higher, rain down on him.

Elephant, worn out, slides (plowing the moss and earth so deeply that the nearby stream pours in at once, and makes a baby brook) to a stop under a tree.

Under what tree, do you think?

Yes, you are right. Under Apple's tree.

Apple leans over so far, to look, that he loses his balance and goes swishing down through the leaves, taking so many with him that he lands on a fine green cushion when he lands on Elephant's back— fortunately, for elephant hairs are as stiff and sharp as darning needles.

Oh, if Apple were only a mahout, like that mahout in India who drives Elephant's Great-Uncle Jumbo! Then Apple could sit on Elephant's neck, soothing with the secret words mahouts and elephants know, and guiding with the pressure of his feet.

But Apple is not a mahout.

Nor is he a mouse, although Elephant thinks he is.

The mouse has caught me! Elephant thinks.

The strength of terror surges through him, and he is crashing and trumpeting onward again, unaware that our astonished hero is on him and that sleeping Caterpillar, still fastened by his strong silk threads, is on our hero.

And what has become of meadow mouse, the cause of all the commotion?

Safe in the mousehole in a tangle of little gray velvet brothers and

Medicine Man Mud-On-His-Moccasins lands on moss and Maiden-hair ferns and mushrooms, while his Medicine Hat and his moccasins rain down on him, and a mouse hurries into its mousehole.

sisters, whisker to whisker and tail lovingly looped around tail, she is peacefully sleeping.

If you told her that because of her

an elephant had been frightened out of his wits, and

a marabou stork and a macaw had been frightened nearly out of
their feathers, and

two ladies had kissed and made up after a misunderstanding, and

a motmot from the Zoo had gone into hiding, and

an old Indian had been frightened out of his moccasins and his
medicine hat, and is sitting on the moss saying "Ugh! Ugh!" and

a new brook is babbling through the forest, and

a boy and a caterpillar have been rescued from a treetop and are
riding off into the unknown,

I don't believe she would know what you were talking about.

N

Let us leave Appleby awhile.
I'd really like to tell a-
Bout the life that brings a smile
To Apple's kind Aunt Bella.

I'd really like to, but I can't just now, since Aunt Bella, usually a happy lady, is feeling that life isn't anything to smile about—night falling, nobody home except herself and her pets, and a strange noise going on outside, making her nervous.

Rumble rumble rumble, goes the noise. RUMBLE RRRRRRR RRUMBLE.

Aunt Bella likes noise when someone she knows is having fun making it, when Uncle Francis is hammering nails, making a little wagon for Nanny the goat to pull, or a house for the wrens, or when Cousin Kate or Pussy the cat are singing, or when Apple is blowing his horn and beating his drum.

"Dear child, always having fun!" she thinks, for little does she know what is happening to Apple at this moment. Little do we know, either.

"Children are always happy," she says to Pussy, forgetting how unhappy children are, sometimes, forgetting how often she used to say, long ago, "I wish I were grown-up! Then I could do whatever I wanted to. Grown-ups are always happy."

Now she only remembers how happy she was when she was a child, and she and Ella had their kind nurse, Nora, to take care of them.

Rumble RUMBLE RRRRRRRRRRRRUMBLE rumble, goes the noise she doesn't like, and Aunt Bella trembles, and wishes she had someone to take care of her now.

Peep from the window, and you will see the rumbler, but please don't let him see you.

He is Leo the lion, looking for his supper.

Now he moves away. *Sniff!* He is on the trail of something. *Sniff!* He leaps on a little green goat wagon under the cherry tree.

But no goat is hitched to it, and, lashing his tail in disappointed fury, Leo leaves. There—*Swish!*—goes the tip of his tail through the bean rows.

Apple often rode in this goat wagon in the peaceful days, such as yesterday and last Saturday, before he took to elephant-riding. Uncle Francis painted it green with some paint Cousin Kate had left over from painting her bathtub green because she means to keep her goldfish in it next winter, and thinks green is most becoming to them. The goldfish, still waving their beautiful tails in Cousin Lucy's lily pond, are named Goldy, Bumboldy, Teeoldy, and Gofoldy.

If only Apple and Caterpillar were in the goat wagon now, with

85

Little Ella and her Elephant and little Bella and her baby-doll with Nurse Nora.

Nanny goat pulling them, they would soon be out of the dark woods and safe from Crocodile and other dangers—although they might meet Leo the lion. But they aren't; the wagon is empty, except for a caterpillar, not Apple's friend, who fell off a bush of the yellow noisette roses called Cloth-of-Gold that Uncle Francis was moving from Cousin Lucy's garden to his own. He is eating a sweet-smelling rose petal (the caterpillar, not Uncle Francis).

What Apple's Caterpillar is doing I can't tell you.

But I can tell you what Nanny goat is doing. She is strolling down a lonely lane with a lily between her lips.

Nanny is having a peaceful time under a tree full of nuts. She has dropped Cousin Kate's blue wool wig, and a nuthatch is taking some of it to another nuthatch, thinking it is something new for supper. Still another nuthatch is wondering what sort of a nest it is, and two more like their own nest too much to pay attention to anything else.

Nanny was wandering here and there, and happened to find Cousin Kate's blue wool wig lying under a window, and ate a strand or two, but found it dry, so she wandered on, dangling it from her mouth, and presently tossed it into a hedge.

A nuthatch upside down on a branch, like a fly on a ceiling, turns his head to look at the wig with interest. Everything interests nuthatches. But he doesn't want it for a nest. He and his mate have pecked a hole in a tree and lined it with feathers and moss, and she is sitting there this minute on a nestful of white eggs speckled with lilac and red. So that when a pair of robins find the blue wig, the nuthatch only gives a cheerful chirp and flies away.

Probably there will be four blue robins' eggs in the wig soon.

Next, Nanny found a lace handkerchief lying in the lane. That was as easy to eat as a lettuce leaf, although not as crisp. Now she has found a broken lily, but is in no hurry to eat it. The wool from the wig, and the handkerchief, have taken the edge from her appetite.

Who has been shedding lace handkerchiefs and broken lilies along the lane?

You know as well as I do; Jocko, of course. And, although it is growing too dark to be certain, isn't that a familiar face peeping down from a nut tree at Nanny?

It is, indeed! Jocko drops on Nanny goat's back as neatly as Apple dropped on Elephant's back, only Jocko does it on purpose.

For once in her life Nanny is surprised instead of surprising.

She shoots forward, while Jocko holds tight.

Mr. and Mrs. Noddy, Aunt Bella's and Uncle Francis' nearest neighbors, are strolling down the narrow lane. They are always nice and neat; Mr. Noddy wears a high silk hat and Mrs. Noddy wears white kid gloves. They are kind, but they get things mixed. Mrs. Noddy heard about Cousin Lucy's cold, but got mixed and told Mr. Noddy that Cousin Kate was ill, and then he got mixed and told her that it was Aunt Ella. They are on their way to inquire for Aunt Bella's health

88

Her nearest neighbors, Mr. and Mrs. Noddy, are taking a nosegay of narcissus to Aunt Bella. They are nice and neat, and Mr. Noddy has a noisette rosebud in his buttonhole, and, in his pocket, a new handkerchief that will never touch his nose. A night-moth flies over the nosegay.

(that's who they think has a cold—or perhaps a sprained ankle—or maybe something else—by now) and take her a nosegay of narcissus.

"Never have I known a more peaceful night," says Mr. Noddy, and, with that—*WHOOSH!*—Nanny tears past with Jocko crouched low on her back, using a twig for a whip.

Mr. and Mrs. Noddy go everywhere together, and now they go backward into the ditch together. Mr. Noddy's high silk hat flies one way, Mrs. Noddy's nosegay another. They have fallen with their feet higher than their heads, and are feeling upset.

Nanny Goat tears past, and Mr. and Mrs. Noddy feel upset.

O

Do come back to our Appleby!
Why will you wander so?
The heavenly orb is rising—see!
(That means the moon, you know.)

It is easy enough to say, Come back to Appleby, but how can we when we can't see him anywhere?

We can see the moon, however. No, those are not ears on either side of the moon's smiling face—only Elephant has ears as big as that. They are clouds.

What does the moon see?

It sees a high silk hat and a nosegay of white narcissus lying in a ditch, forgotten by Mr. and Mrs. Noddy, who forgot, also, where they had meant to go, and have gone home.

It sees a mother opossum playing with her baby opossums.

It sees an ostrich running as fast as it can; it had its head buried in sand when Elephant's party left the Zoo, and is hurrying to catch up with the others.

It sees hundreds of owls.

It sees tired Uncle Francis trudging through the osiers (or willows, if you like—same thing) toward home. It sees Common Silverside in the water in Uncle Francis' hat. It sees itself in the water, too, and in Cousin Lucy's lily pond where Goldy, Bumboldy, Teeoldy, and Gofoldy, the goldfish, drift and dream, and in dew on the daisy that the

91

mouse hid under, and in the stream that led Apple into the deep, dark woods, and in other streams and lakes and in the faraway ocean.

The moon sees Jocko on Nanny goat, having fun, showing off to himself, riding backward, riding standing on his head, riding without holding on. And, walking slowly toward Nanny and Jocko, playing "O Sole Mio" on a hand organ, the moon sees the Italian gentleman named Signor Olivetto, who appears to be looking for something or somebody.

"Who?" the owls cry, to the moon or to one another. "O-o-oh, Who-o, Who-o, Who-o-o-o?"

Jocko sees Signor Olivetto, and knows who he is looking for, and jumps off Nanny goat and runs as fast as he can, back down the lane. But he has to stop and pay attention to so many interesting things—a bat, a moth, a button bright with moonlight, and the tip of his own tail—that all of a sudden he hears "The Wearing of the Green" (that is the tune Signor Olivetto is playing on his hand organ now) almost on top of him, and just has time to leap into the ditch, where Mrs. Noddy's nosegay and Mr. Noddy's high silk hat are lying.

Jocko likes Signor Olivetto, and means to go back to him after a while and let him do all the work of playing the organ while Jocko has the fun of collecting pennies, but he doesn't think Signor Olivetto has had a long enough holiday yet.

Now the moon sees Mr. Noddy's hat rise from the ditch all by itself—no, two paws lift it, a small, anxious face looks after Signor Olivetto. Then the hat comes down like a lid and sinks into the ditch.

The moon sees all these things. But it cannot see through the woven green roof of the forest. Anything may be happening there, for all we and the moon know.

By the way, speaking of ears—oh, yes, we were, when we were speaking of the moon—I once heard of a little boy with such big, stand-out ears that every night when he went to bed they would act like springs and make his head bounce up and down each time it struck the pillow.

Signor Olivetto the Organ-grinder stops playing "O Sole Mio" on his organ, and sheds a few tears for missing Jocko. He thinks he is alone, but the heavenly Orb (the Moon) and some owls look down at him, an opossum and her baby opossums look up at him, an owlet moth flies near, and behind him an ostrich with an orange part way down its throat runs in search of its friends from the Zoo.

P

The Moon is big and beauteous,
It silvers pig and peak,
And yet I'd rather far be us,
For we can walk and speak.

The moon cannot see through the woven green roof of the forest, and neither could we if we were dropping from the sky with a parachute.

The moon cannot say, "Let's walk into the forest," and walk there, as we are doing.

Hark! Someone is coming through the whispering pines and the hemlocks. Can it be Apple?

No, it can't; it is Pinkfeather, Deerfoot's squaw, with their papoose Fawnfoot on her back, going home to supper after a pleasant powwow with her mother, Squaw Prickly Pear (an Indian lady who is named after a cactus with sharp prickles and pretty yellow flowers).

Now even Pinkfeather and her papoose have disappeared, and we are alone with the silence. At least, I hope we are alone, but we'd better not loiter, I think.

The moon can silver pig and peak and plenty of other things, such as Mrs. Noddy's nosegay, the button that interested Jocko, Jocko himself (or, at least, his tail and his paws, all that show from under Mr. Noddy's hat), the ocean, Common Silverside in Uncle Francis' hat, and anything else its silver beams fall upon.

Squaw Prickly Pear parts from Pinkfeather and her Papoose after a pleasant powwow. A Peacock butterfly—not the you-know-what butterfly that we want—flutters over the petals of a cactus called Prickly Pear. This potted plant was a present from a friend named Princess Prairie-Chicken.

We can't do that. But I still say I'd rather far be us.

The particular peak the moon is turning to silver is Mud-on-His-Moccasin's mountain home, which I daresay he is wishing he had never left.

The particular pig the moon is turning to silver is rooting up the pansies in Cousin Lucy's pansy bed. She is so proud of them that she took a photograph of Apple looking at them, and, although she didn't hold the camera quite right, gave copies to all the family.

Cousin Kate said, "It's a pity you cut off Apple's head."

Aunt Bella said, "How pretty!" and pasted hers into her photograph album on the page with the photograph of Apple's parents and an early picture of Apple being pushed in his perambulator by his proud papa.

Aunt Bella is fond of family portraits. A painting in her parlor is of her great-great-great-grandparents. The lady is in a poke bonnet that hides her as much as Mr. Noddy's hat hid Jocko, so that we can't tell whether she is pretty or plain. It is easy to tell about the gentleman, who wears a periwig.

But to get back to the pig in the pansy bed; it roots up as many plants as it pleases, and then trots down the lane—that lane we know so well, where now the evening primroses are wide open and wet with pearls of dew—and into Cousin Clement's parterre.

How much is packed into that one word, parterre! Either you can say, "A flower garden with beds in a pattern separated by walks," or you can save your breath and save your time and say "parterre," and mean exactly the same thing.

Cousin Clement's parterre is a pleasant place. In the center is a pavilion made of the woven branches of a peach tree, a plum tree, a pear tree, and a pecan tree. In summer you can sit here and eat peaches, pears, and plums, and in autumn, when the nuts ripen, you can eat pecans, by putting out your hand to pick them. You can sit here and

A Page from Aunt Bella's Photograph Album ⟶

1. Apple's Parents ready for a fancy-dress party, in a Periwig and a Poke bonnet with a plume, like the people in the portraits.

2. When Apple was a baby he was pushed in his perambulator by his proud Papa past the penguin pond in the Park. The puppy came to protect them.

3. Cousin Lucy's photograph of her Pansies, with a Parnassus butterfly among them, and Apple looking at them. Under the plum tree two pouter pigeons are parading, and one of Cousin Clement's peacocks perches on the wall.

4. An empty place! What a pity! Please paste in a picture, or make one with pencil or paint.

P. Pesky
Photographer

1

2

3

4

eat oranges and bananas, too, but you will have to bring those with you.

Someone has been sitting here lately, and left a pile of peach stones and a colored picture book. The breeze turns the pages for us; here is a view of Polar regions, all ice pinnacles and Northern Lights, here is a pink Persian palace with a flock of green parakeets flying past, here is a pirate with a parrot on his shoulder.

I think it must have been Apple who was here; this morning, perhaps.

Where is Apple this evening?

In front of the pavilion is a pond, that looks now like an enormous moonlight-colored butterfly. Brilliant-colored Chinese fish of Paradise, whose other name is butterfly fish (trust Cousin Clement!), swim here, and, in the spring, plenty of polliwogs. Around the pond are flower beds, butterfly-shaped like the pond, packed with peonies, pinks, poppies, petunias, and phlox, and close to the ground grow portulacas with pretty cups of every color, bright as wet paint.

When it is daylight you can hardly see the petals for the real butterflies fluttering above them.

Now what has become of that pig? While we were looking at the parterre he ate some plums that had fallen on a path, but where is he now?

Perhaps he has gone to root among potatoes and parsley and the pumpkin vines where the biggest pumpkin will be saved to make a Halloween jack-o'-lantern, Apple hopes.

No, I can't see the pig. Can you?

We can see Caleb, though. Hotspur the horse has brought him and the calash safely home. Caleb still sleeps on. The pigeons came cooing, expecting him to feed them with parched peas; they perched all over the calash and him, holding on with their pink feet. A pouter pigeon perched on Hotspur. The peacocks came, trailing their plumes of purple and green and fiery gold.

Caleb slept on.

Now the pigeons and peacocks sleep, too, heads under wings, and even poor Hotspur has decided he will have to be patient about getting his supper, and is dozing, although his head, of course, is out in the evening air.

Don't let us wake them. Help yourself to a peach, Cousin Clement would want you to, and come back to the lane, where Jocko is still hiding in the ditch.

Look! He is venturing out.

He likes his new hat so much that he wears it, although he has to use both paws to hold it up so that he can see.

He sees two gentlemen. One of them is Uncle Francis, and one is Mr. Perkins the postman with his postbag on his back. Uncle Francis is showing him Common Silverside, fully recovered and swimming around in the hat, and Mr. Perkins is very much interested, for he is fond of all animals and has many pets himself. He has quite a pack of dogs, a poodle, a Pekingese, a Pomeranian, and plenty of puppies; he has a parrot named Polly, and a donkey named Paddy. At Christmas-time Mr. Perkins puts panniers on Paddy and fills them with packages (Christmas presents, of course), and they make their rounds together.

Jocko sees Mr. Perkins and Uncle Francis, and then he sees something else, and smells it and hears it, too.

Snuffle snuffle snuffle, wheeze wheeze wheeze, and a patter of paws.

At last! I told you Quentin the pug was somewhere, and here he is, running as fast as he can, which isn't very fast, for he is portly, to meet Uncle Francis.

Poor Jocko thinks Quentin is after him. He drops Mr. Noddy's hat and runs to Mr. Perkins, just pausing to pull Apple's shining stone out of his pocket, to throw at the pug. A piece of paper comes with it, and falls to the ground. Then Jocko runs up Mr. Perkins and jumps into his postbag.

If Quentin has one trick—and he has, exactly one—it is retrieving. Throw anything, Quentin will bring it back to you. Try to play croquet

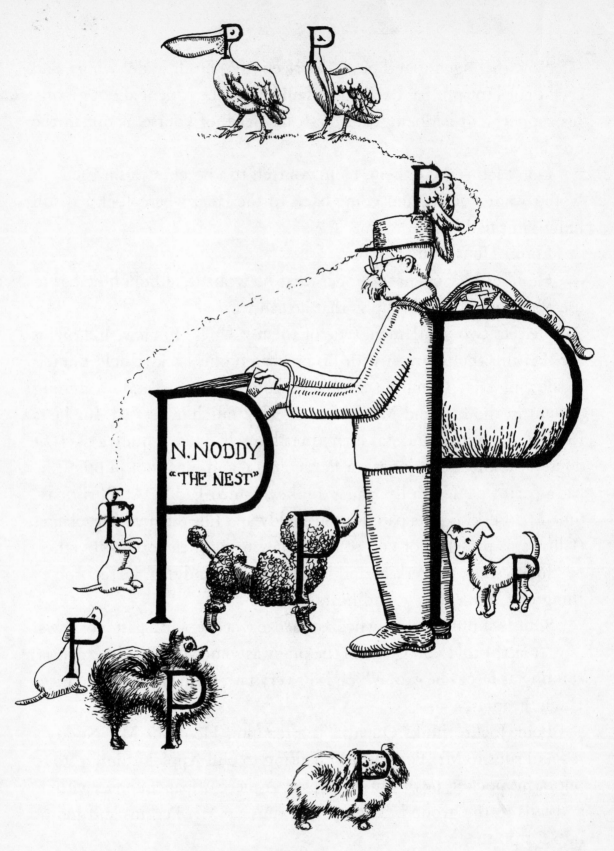

Patient Mr. Perkins the Postman, with his post-bag, at a postbox,
with some of his pets—Prunella the Poodle, Puff the Pomeranian,
Pitty-Sing the Pekingese, Plish, Plum and Paddlecake the puppies,
and Polly the Parrot, who is pretending not to see a pair of Pelicans
from the Zoo passing.

with Quentin watching. Back he will bring every ball you hit. Or try to throw something away, and see whether Quentin will let you.

Now he brings Apple's stone to try to give it back to Jocko. But there is nothing to be seen of Jocko except one bright eye looking out from under the flap of the postbag.

"I think something ran up my back!" cries Mr. Perkins, but Uncle Francis is bending to pick up the paper and pays no attention.

"A note! Now where did this come from?"

"Something *did* run up my back!"

"I don't see a thing," says Uncle Francis. "Who do you suppose this note is for?"

"Something *did*— It says 'For Anybody,' so it must be for you."

"But I'm not Anybody. I'm Somebody."

"Well—yes—" says Mr. Perkins.

And they both begin to guess who the note is from, and who it is for, and what is inside.

Cousin Lucy is like that. She will try to guess who has written her a letter; sometimes she can't guess for days. Once it took her two weeks before she guessed "Ella!" Then she opened the letter, and Aunt Ella had written, "Won't you come to my party tomorrow?" Cousin Lucy had to write, "I am so sorry that I can't come to your party last week."

Now Uncle Francis opens the note. You know what is there for him to read.

" '*Dear Everybody,*' "

"Oh, then it's for me, too," says Mr. Perkins.

" '*I take my*' something '*in hand*'—I can't read this word. Look, Mr. Perkins, is it penguin?"

"Is it pelican? A pelican would be very large to take in one hand."

"Oh, it is pencil! '*I take my pencil in hand to tell you that I am lost up a tree*—' Now, who could be lost up a tree?"

"Your cat? You have to climb after her quite often."

"But I don't think Pussy can write. Let's see—'*up a tree and am surrounded by a Crocodile who snaps his jaws at me.*' "

101

Common Silverside leaps in the hat, splashing moonlight and water.

"Dear me! What's the matter with you, my little fish? Mr. Perkins, that fish understands every word I say. Let's see, where were we—?"

"'*Up a tree.*'"

"Oh, yes! '*If it is not too much trouble, would you kindly rescue me? I am very much upset. Hoping you are the same, I am your loving—*'"

Mr. Perkins can't wait. He peers over Uncle Francis' shoulder, and they shout together:

"'*Apple*'!"

Q

Quick! Quick! Come, let us join the Quest!
Come! Through the woods we'll scramble
And seek our hero east and west,
Though torn by thorn and bramble.

"We must form a searching party!" cries Uncle Francis, and Mr. Perkins answers, "We must, indeed!"

Uncle Francis runs one way, Mr. Perkins another. Quentin and Common Silverside go with Uncle Francis. Jocko follows Mr. Perkins, although neither of them know it. Mr. Perkins doesn't know that Jocko is in the postbag, and Jocko, tired from excitement, is fast asleep.

When Uncle Francis tells Aunt Bella the news, she is so startled that she throws the family portraits out of the window, as though the house were on fire. He just has time to save the teapot with the blue Chinaman.

"Bella, my dear, be calm!"

So Aunt Bella is calm.

"Let us start at once," she says. "I shan't have a moment of quietness until I see our dear Apple with my own two eyes."

Uncle Francis looks quickly. Yes, two eyes. Aunt Bella has counted correctly. Now he turns his mind to the quest for Apple.

"Bloodhounds," he says. "We must trace Apple with bloodhounds."

But, although they look everywhere, they can't find a single bloodhound, and have to be contented with Quentin, who is now fast asleep with the Apple-Jocko stone beside him, and is dreaming about having a quail for supper. He doesn't want to wake, and is sleepy and cross, and has to be prodded from behind with Uncle Francis' umbrella in the most unbloodhound-like manner.

He does remember to take the stone to return, in case he meets Jocko.

Uncle Francis takes his umbrella in case of rain, a lantern in case the woods are dark, and a quilt in case the night grows cold.

Aunt Bella takes a glass of quince jelly, just in case.

"We can stop for Ella and Lucy and Kate and some of the more intimate friends of the family on our way," says Uncle Francis.

Mr. Perkins is waiting for them, and so is Jocko, still asleep and hidden in the postbag.

"Caleb told me Apple was in the calash with Cousin Clement," Aunt Ella says, when they stop for her.

"He told me that, too!" cries Aunt Bella.

But Caleb, when they at last succeed in waking him, is so surprised at being home instead of being at the edge of the woods waiting for Cousin Clement that he doesn't know anything about anything. Also, he is so sleepy that he goes on nodding.

"Caleb, do you know where Apple is?"

Caleb nods.

"Is he safe?"

Quentin the pug is fast asleep on a quilt, and does not see the Quetzal in the Quince tree nor the Quail quickly walking away. The roses are the kind called Ami (French for friend, you know) Quinard, and the butterfly above them is called the Queen. The lady in the painting is a Queen, too. Under her you see a picture of quacking wild ducks in a quiet sky.

Caleb nods.

"Oh, what a relief! Will you lead us to him, please?"

Caleb nods, and lets out a loud snore.

"Caleb, wake up! Wake up! Oh, if we only had Kate with us!"

"*I* can make as much noise as Kate. Stand back, everyone. Put your fingers in your ears," Aunt Ella orders, and roars:

"W-A-A-Y-*KUP*!"

You can hear ripe peaches, pears, and plums thud-thud-thudding from the trees in the parterre. Petals fall in a snowstorm from a climbing white rose. Hotspur jerks up his head and whinnies. Peacocks scream, pigeons fly away. Jocko quivers and quakes and lifts the flap of the postbag to peep out.

Caleb sleeps on.

After waiting hopefully for a moment, they tiptoe away.

Aunt Ella is blushing and hanging her head, and resolving never to boast again. Aunt Bella whispers, "It was wonderful, Ella!" But even that doesn't cheer her.

They stop for Cousin Kate and Cousin Lucy. Mr. Rollo Roberts, who happens to be calling on Cousin Lucy, also joins the party, pausing at his own house to fill his high silk hat with things that may be useful, while the others wait impatiently, and some even shout, "Hurry! Hurry!"

"My advice is, never hurry and never worry," advises Mr. Roberts, coming out, not hurrying and not worrying, with a rug and a raincoat over one arm, his rubbers on his feet, and as many fresh buttered rolls (wrapped in wax paper) as his pockets will hold. "Or, if anyone does worry, let him or her remember how fortunate it is that Appleby isn't quintuplets, or he or she would have to worry five times as much."

In one hand Mr. Roberts holds a reference book called *How To Tell the Birds,* in case anyone should see a bird in the woods.

"How to tell the birds what?" asks Uncle Francis.

But Mr. Roberts does not hear him, for he is offering Cousin Lucy what he holds in his other hand. It is one perfect rose, the kind that is called Red Radiance, if you care. Indeed, it is called Red Radiance even if you don't care.

"Oh, Mr. Roberts! For *me*?" cries Cousin Lucy.

"Certainly not! It's for Quentin," Cousin Kate mutters crossly. " 'For *me*?' How silly!"

Mr. Roberts, pretending not to hear, bows to Cousin Lucy, lifts his hat, and—

Rattle! Patter! Plop!

Out fall the rest of the things he has brought.

Some raisins.

Some radishes.

Some rice.

A cake of rose-geranium soap, in case anyone's hands or face get dirty in the woods.

A railroad timetable, in case they come to a railroad station.

It is easy to find the railroad timetable, the rose-geranium soap, and a few of the radishes. But the rice is scattered everywhere (birds will find it for breakfast) and the raisins are invisible in the dusk. So that Mr. Roberts has to return to his kitchen to repack his hat, not hurrying and not worrying, while Uncle Francis dances with impatience, and Aunt Bella says, "Francis, my dear, be calm."

Since Mr. Roberts has no more rice or raisins left, he fills the spaces in his hat with ripe red raspberries.

On the advice of Aunt Ella, Cousin Kate, Uncle Francis, and Mr. Perkins, he fastens his hat with a muffler tied under his chin, for he is so polite that otherwise he would be sure to take it off every time anyone spoke to him, and we know what would happen then.

Now he says, "Shall we start? Is anything detaining us?"

"Oh!" cries forgetful Uncle Francis. "I forgot to bring some quinine, in case any of us gets chills and fever. I'll just dash quickly home—"

Aunt Bella quiets him by saying they won't be going into any swamps, where they would be likely to catch such things.

Little does she know!

The word "catch" reminds Uncle Francis that he has forgotten his fishing rod and some breadcrumbs, in case there is a chance to catch some fish—and then let them go, of course.

But one and all discourage him from returning for these. So he, in his turn, says, "Shall we start?"

They start—and high time, too.

They pause to invite Mr. and Mrs. Noddy to go, just to be polite.

But Mr. and Mrs. Noddy, although they are shocked by the news—Mrs. Noddy cries "*No!*" and Mr. Noddy soothingly says, "Now, now, now!"—are still feeling too upset to come.

"We were upset in a ditch by a galloping goat with a little boy riding it," Mr. Noddy explains.

"Nanny and Apple!" cry their callers.

"Which way did they go? It is very important when you wish to find someone to know where to go," says Mr. Roberts.

"That way!" Mr. and Mrs. Noddy point, one east, one west, then, each feeling that the other must be right, their arms cross as they point, one west, one east.

Off goes everyone, too excited to hear Mr. Noddy calling, "He was a very *little* little boy, in a red cap and jacket," and Mrs. Noddy adding, "And he had a long tail."

"Follow me, please," says Uncle Francis, leading them along the stream where lately he was running up and down with Common Silverside. "This way. Quiet, please."

Cousin Lucy screams.

"I saw a chimpanzee behind that willow!"

"Nonsense, my dear. We are all a little excited."

"Impossible, Lucy. I thought I saw a giraffe in the meadow, but that is impossible, too. We are all excited, and moonlight plays queer tricks."

"Impossible indeed, Miss Kate," agrees Mr. Roberts, who is trying to make himself believe that the hippopotamus (our old friend with the smile) he saw before it sank was only a turtle.

They enter the woods, followed at a polite distance by Giraffe and Chimpanzee and several other interested animals from the Zoo. Hippopotamus watches them go, his eyes sticking out of his head and shining in the moonlight liked sucked lollipops.

Now the searching party skirts the swamp.

Cousin Lucy screams again, but in a pleased way.

"A clue!" she cries, for in a circle of lantern light she sees the pink petals of an arethusa, the very one that Apple gathered for Aunt Bella and then dropped. "Someone has passed this way!"

Mr. Roberts stubs his toe on the next clue. It is the wooden decoy duck that Deerfoot wasted an arrow on, and that Sir Droppit the dog retrieved and dropped.

They gather around it, and all agree that, like the broken flower, it is a clue, but no one knows to what.

They come to a place where the trail branches into three trails.

"This way! Follow me!" cries Uncle Francis, starting along one.

At the very same moment, Mr. Roberts says, "My advice is to follow this one," and starts along another, while Mr. Perkins starts along the third, crying, "Ready, set, go, ladies and gentlemen!"

"Who is leader?" asks Cousin Kate.

"Francis," says Aunt Bella; "Mr. Roberts," murmurs Cousin Lucy; and "Mr. Perkins," says Aunt Ella (just so that everyone will have a vote) and adds, "But I am perfectly willing to be." All three speak at once. This is growing very confusing.

"My advice is, that we count out," advises Mr. Roberts. "Do you prefer 'My Mother Told Me' or 'Into the Middle of the Deep Blue Sea'?"

"But, first, which lady shall do the counting out?"

"Let the ladies draw pieces of grass, with the shortest piece winning."

"But who shall hold the grass for the ladies?"

"COME ON!" shouts Cousin Kate. "Quentin has decided! Quentin is leading us!"

Indeed, for the first and probably the last time, Quentin the pug has waddled ahead of the others. Peace is restored, and they, and you and I, follow him along the forest trail.

I seem to know it, don't you?

When were we here before?

Oh, I remember! When we saw Pinkfeather and her papoose Fawnfoot going home from their day with Squaw Prickly Pear.

Pinkfeather and Fawnfoot have reached their wigwam now, and are hungry. Pinkfeather wonders what Deerfoot has brought back for supper from his hunting.

As we know, he hasn't brought a thing.

Pinkfeather is quite annoyed.

"That's queer," she says, and takes a quail quill and writes a list for him to get from the store at the other side of the woods.

> 1 lb. best bacon
> 1 doz. strictly fresh eggs
> 1 qt. milk for Fawnfoot
> 1 bone for Sir Droppit

"Quick, quick!" she cries.

As Deerfoot, followed by Droppit, hurries on his errand, wild ducks fly overhead in the quiet moonlight, crying, "Quack! Quack! Quack!"

Deerfoot has refilled his quiver, but he isn't going to waste an arrow on them again.

"Can't fool me twice!" he calls up to them. "I know what you are, you old decoys, you!"

"*Quack!*" cry the ducks, and fly out of sight.

"Deerfoot, old fellow!" exclaims a well-known voice.

It is his cousin Gumbo, who has decided he simply must have something solid to eat before he goes to bed, and is also on his way to the store for bacon and eggs. But he is not going to tell Deerfoot where he is going if he can help it.

And Deerfoot isn't going to tell Gumbo where he is going if he can help it.

"Gumbo, old fellow! I wish I could ask you to come back to supper, but you know what an appetite hunting gives one, and I haven't even a bit of left-over buffalo."

Buffalo! thinks Gumbo. And I with my old grapes and mushrooms!

"Don't give it another thought," he says. "When one eats a whole bear, it doesn't leave room for even the best buffalo."

Bear! thinks Deerfoot. And I with my old berries and edible roots!

They stroll along together, stealing glances at each other, each thinking, "How! How! How can I get away from him and reach the store to buy bacon and eggs before it closes?"

Then they stand still. Then they drop to their knees and put their ears to the ground.

A strange sound is stealing through the woods.

"Ugh! Ugh! Ugh! Ugh! Ugh!"

They creep beneath the whispering pines and the hemlocks, shading their eyes with their hands (simply from habit; only a little moonlight sifts through the branches). They move quietly as shadows; not a leaf rustles, not a twig snaps, nothing breaks the silence except a loud *"Ouch!"* from Gumbo when a wild-rose bush scratches him, and the mysterious "Ugh! Ugh! Ugh!"

"Why, Grandfather!" they cry together. "How in the world did *you* get here?"

For there, surrounded by maidenhair fern, his moccasins, and his medicine hat, sits old Medicine Man Mud-on-His-Moccasins, still saying, "Ugh! Ugh!" in a rather absent-minded way by now.

He tells them how he meant to surprise them, and how an earthquake knocked him down (that is what he has decided Elephant was).

They have so much to talk about that Deerfoot and Gumbo forget time and bacon and eggs. Mud-on-His-Moccasins still has some of the provisions for his journey from the mountains, and they have a fine supper.

"Must shove it down somehow—can't hurt the old gentleman's feelings," Deerfoot mumbles, showing off to Gumbo.

"I'll pretend to nibble—have to be polite—" Gumbo whispers to Deerfoot, as well as he can with his mouth too full.

Mud-on-His-Moccasins is so tired, and Deerfoot and Gumbo are so full of food, that all three fall asleep, propped against a pine tree and each other.

Sir Droppit the dog, weary from wagging his tail in thanks for many delicious morsels, is turning around and around, making a bed for himself at their feet, when, suddenly, you can see that he hears something. His floppy ears, that look like a couple of pancakes, twitch and quiver, his moist black nose twitches and quivers, and—

Where is he? He was here a second ago; the ferns are still shaking.

I know what I hope. I hope he is behaving more like a bloodhound than Quentin is, and has caught scent of Apple. Of course it could be Cousin Clement, or the crocodile, or any of Elephant's friends, such as that rare bird with the beautiful green and vermilion feathers, the quetzal, or just a stay-at-home-here-in-his-own-woods rabbit, but I hope it is Apple.

It's time someone found Apple.

R

What perils lie in wait ahead!
How deep the woods, how still!
Yet calmly on our searchers tread!
With heads held high, until—!

Sometimes our searchers can only see what the bobbing circle of lantern light shows—moss, moths, the bright eyes of a startled squirrel, and, once, another clue, a tiny blue bracelet of Indian beads. (My guess about this is that Squaw Prickly Pear gave it to her grandson, the papoose Fawnfoot, and that Fawnfoot dropped it on the way to his father's wigwam. This is only a guess. What is your guess?)

Sometimes they come to a clearing and find that the moon is traveling with them.

Mr. Roberts is entertaining them with bird calls that he finds in his reference book (you remember, *How To Tell the Birds*).

He croaks like a raven.

He whistles like a redbird, and then says, "Clucky-tucky-tuk," because that is what his bird book says is the redbird's call. The bird book is probably right, yet it sounds to me exactly like Mr. Roberts saying, "Clucky-tucky-tuk."

He twitters like a redpoll, he sings like a robin, and he taps his hat with his finger to sound like a redheaded woodpecker.

Cousin Kate can do bird calls, too, and crows like a rooster to prove it, making many a rooster crow in answer, from farms too far away for

Mr. Rollo Roberts puts on his rubbers, takes his rug and his raincoat, and is ready to rush to the rescue. He is doing bird calls he learned from his Reference book, "How to Tell the Birds," and has roused two rabbits hiding in a clump of rattlesnake fern, a Redheaded woodpecker, some robins, and one Redpoll. The other Redpoll thinks this is ridiculous, and refuses to notice Mr. Roberts.

her to hear them, and making Uncle Francis cry, "I forgot to feed the chickens!"

Aunt Bella is happy to tell him that she fed them.

Aunt Bella feels peaceful because she is sure that, with Uncle Francis here, everything is going to be all right.

Cousin Lucy is sure that, with Mr. Roberts here, everything is going to be all right.

Aunt Ella is sure that as long as she herself is here, everything is going to be all right.

It has begun to seem to them all half a picnic and half a dream, and I think they have almost forgotten what brought them here.

Jocko lifts the flap and leans out of Mr. Perkins' postbag as though he were leaning out of a window, dreamily waving now and then at his distant cousin Chimpanzee, coming along through the branches, dreamily gazing now and then at Quentin, waddling far behind again, moonlight sometimes striking a diamond flash from the stone he still carries in his mouth.

Animals join the party, drawn by lantern light, curiosity, lostness, or friendliness. It begins to seem no stranger to see a giraffe's tall dappled neck than to see the moonlight-dappled trunk of a tall tree. Kangaroo, with her baby in her pouch, hops beside Cousin Kate in her wild-woods wool wig—scarlet wool with a little flag stuck in the top that says "Positively No Hunting, Shooting, or Fishing," so that it wouldn't have been of any use to him if Uncle Francis had remembered his fishing rod —and neither one seems surprised at the company she is keeping.

Calmly on our searchers go, with heads held high, until—
Swish! *Crash!*

Uncle Francis, who has managed to get in the lead, finds the fourth clue, the silver birch tree, torn up by Elephant as a present to Deerfoot, and left across the trail.

It trips him, he falls on his face (saved from harm by the springy, leafy branches), and

Swish! Crash!

Swish! Crash!

Swish! Crash!

Swish! Crash!

Swish! Crash!

(Let me see, have we the correct number of Swish! Crash!es? Aunt Bella, Aunt Ella, Cousin Lucy, Cousin Kate, Mr. Perkins—oh, one more for Mr. Roberts!)

Swish! Crash!

They all trip over the fourth clue and one another.

Cousin Kate's wild-woods wig flies in one direction; Mr. Roberts' hat, in spite of the tying-on muffler, flies in another. A very young rabbit, resting under the roots of the fourth clue, is hit by the rose-geranium soap, and races back to his burrow, sure that it was a falling star.

Everyone else lies comfortably among the birch branches or on cushions of moss, enjoying the rest, except Jocko, who has sprung to a tree (one with its roots still in the ground) and hangs by his tail from a branch, and Quentin, who now has a chance to catch up with the party, and, at last, return the shining stone to Jocko.

Jocko is a surprise to everyone, for, until now, he has been hidden in the postbag, and they all agree that he is a delightful addition to the party.

First he drops on Quentin's back and has a short ride, making everyone laugh except Quentin.

Then he finds Cousin Kate's wig and tries it on, making everyone laugh except Cousin Kate.

Then he bites into one of Mr. Roberts' radishes, and leaps backward as though a wasp had stung him, flinging the radish away, chattering and scolding at it for burning his mouth, making everyone laugh except himself.

Mr. Roberts shares his rolls, spread with Aunt Bella's quince jelly, among them all, not forgetting Quentin and Jocko. This soothes Jocko, and he makes the rounds of the party, shaking hands with everyone.

Aunt Bella feels that they have met before, then decides that surely this polite little monkey could never have pulled out Cockatoo's tail feather.

It is so pleasant and restful that they might be lying there yet if Uncle Francis hadn't given the order, "Forward! March!"

Aunt Bella and Quentin awake from light slumber, Cousin Kate puts on her wig, Jocko seats himself upon Mr. Perkins' shoulder, dropping the shining stone, which poor patient Quentin again picks up.

Mr. Roberts lifts his head from its nest in the birch branches to look for his hat.

Cousin Lucy screams.

"Mr. Roberts! Your head!"

Mr. Roberts' head is a shocking sight indeed. Smashed raspberries cover it; blood-red raspberry juice trickles down his face. And no one but Mr. Roberts knew about the raspberries he packed in his hat, and he has forgotten them.

Putting his hand to his head, then looking by lantern light at his crimson fingers, he turns pale but remains brave.

"You have been scalped," says Aunt Ella. "Indians must have crept upon us while no one was noticing."

"I would have noticed," says Mr. Roberts.

"Probably not. Indians are very quiet," says Uncle Francis.

Mr. Roberts becomes paler and braver.

"Never mind me," he says. "All that matters is to find Appleby."

They all clap such a noble remark. Cousin Lucy binds Mr. Roberts' head with her lace scarf. He finds his rose-geranium soap and puts it in his pocket; plenty of room in his pockets now. Jocko is allowed to carry Mr. Roberts' hat.

I might as well tell you here that he soon throws it at cousin Chimpanzee, who is delighted, having lost Apple's cap long ago.

Uncle Francis repeats, "Forward! March!"

They march forward.

S

So Forward, March, our searchers go,
And also round and round.
They seek him high, they seek him low,
Still Apple is not found.

"This is becoming quite a journey," says Mr. Roberts. "Fortunately, I am very fond of travel." And he begins to tell them about his travels.

Uncle Francis, who is growing rather impatient, says, "Mr. Roberts, do you think this is quite the time?"

Mr. Roberts replies with a low bow, "Quite!"

"Oh, please go on, Mr. Roberts!" begs Cousin Lucy.

Mr. Roberts goes on.

He is telling her about the swans that swim on English rivers, when Cousin Kate sees an enormous snake—a boa constrictor from the Zoo —wound around a tree, and lets out such a shriek that she stops Mr. Roberts and gives Uncle Francis an idea.

"Let us all call Apple at the top of our lungs."

Although no one can be heard through Cousin Kate's call, you can see that not one of them is cheating by the way they all turn red and look about to burst.

Squirrels wake and scamper away. Snails draw in their horns. A seal (from the Zoo, yes, of course, of course, of course) in a distant forest pool claps his flippers and barks. Far, far away in a field beyond the woods, two sparrows that have built their nest in a scarecrow's hat wonder what waked them, since it certainly isn't sunrise.

Then silence surges back like a wave of the sea.

Speaking of the sea reminds me of that old salt, Great-Uncle Thomas. How astonished our friends would be if they knew that at this moment a ship was sailing—or, really, steaming—on the sea, bringing Great-Uncle Thomas nearer to his native shores with every turn of the screw. With him are two friends, who are called the Terrible Turk and the Smiling Sultan.

Please do not speak of this to any of the searching party, as Great-Uncle Thomas wants it to be a surprise.

Now, back to the woods.

"Shall I shout again?" asks Cousin Kate.

"*No!*" cries Uncle Francis. "Silence, please."

"O-o-o-OOO!" howls Quentin, who has sat down to rest on the fifth clue, the ilex, or holly, that Apple tried to climb, and Elephant uprooted for him.

Aunt Bella kindly comforts Quentin, who, after a few sad sniffs, again picks up the stone that he dropped in order to howl.

At almost the same time—one second after Quentin sat on the holly—Mr. Roberts finds the sixth clue, the motto from the Christmas cracker that Apple, or Jocko, dropped, that says:

> *If I should offer you a kiss,*
> *Would that offend you, my dear Miss?*

With a deep bow, he gives it to Cousin Lucy, who lowers her eyelids, blushes, and looks pleased.

"Forward! March!" orders Aunt Ella.

They are growing tired and discouraged, and push on in silence for a long time.

"Oh, where is Apple?" Aunt Bella sighs.

"Oh, where are we?" Mr. Perkins asks.

"We are here, Mr. Perkins."

"But where is here?"

The *Smiling Sultan* takes off his slippers and sits in the sun on the ship's deck. If he is thirsty he can take out the stopper and drink sweet syrup. If he is hungry he can eat strawberries. If he is homesick he can look at the picture of his Home, Sweet Home, with his pet swan swimming in the smooth water. He has a sea gull and a snail for company. The snail is a stowaway; it came aboard hidden in the strawberries.

119

"Here is in the woods, Mr. Perkins."

"But what are we doing?"

"We are looking for Apple, Mr. Perkins."

"We are lost in the woods, and we are going around in a circle," says Mr. Perkins. "We have passed that same sassafras tree six times. I have kept count on my fingers."

"Everyone be calm!" orders Uncle Francis, beginning to shiver and shake.

So everyone is calm except Uncle Francis.

They go on slowly, and, as they go, Cousin Kate pulls strands of red wool from her wig and ties them to branches.

Soon they come to a ravel of red wool on a branch, and know they are still going in a circle.

"Stop!" cries Uncle Francis. "We are indeed lost. Who is leader of this party?"

"Not I!" cry Mr. Roberts and Mr. Perkins together, and Aunt Ella rather unkindly says, "I offered to be, but you said you were, Francis."

Then they stand in silence, with bowed heads and heavy hearts.

Did I say silence? Listen!

What is that rustle in the underbrush?

Why does Quentin drop his stone and begin to sniff?

What is this, with ears like flapping pancakes, that leaps into sight, wriggling all over, wagging his tail, laying his front legs flat and sticking up his behind (his way of bowing) before he leaps on each in turn, with licks from a loving pink tongue and barks of welcome?

T

With blue tattoo upon his chest,
  And bringing friends from Turkey.
Great-Uncle Thomas sails due west
  Through weather clear or murky.

We were talking about the moon. That was quite a long time ago, but it was about this same moon on this same night that we were talking, and about the things it could see and shine on and turn to silver, such as that pig in Cousin Lucy's pansy bed, and the dew on the daisy that Elephant's mouse hid under, and the faraway ocean.

Now we see it turning the whole heaving ocean to silver, and striking silver sparks from a hundred tiny full moons and crescent moons embroidered on the jacket of a gentleman in a turban who stands on the deck of the fairly good ship *Tapioca*. Beside his turban and his moon-embroidered jacket, he wears a sash, a pair of Turkish trousers that look like two beautiful silk laundry bags full of laundry, silver-embroidered slippers that turn up at the toes, a long curved sword that he often trips over, and a pleasant smile.

Perhaps you remember that I asked you not to tell that Great-Uncle Thomas is on his way home, to make a surprise visit, bringing his friends the Terrible Turk and the Smiling Sultan.

The Smiling Sultan is in his stateroom, not smiling just now, because he is seasick, but here is the other gentleman. He likes to be called the

121

Great-Uncle Thomas and The Terrible Turk (in his turban) talk while Timbuc and Timbuctoo, the tame toucans, take the air.

Terrible Turk, and everyone calls him that to please him, for he is so gentle and kind that he makes everyone want to be kind to him.

That jolly old tar, Great-Uncle Thomas, stands beside him, taking such deep breaths of salt air that the little blue mermaid tattooed on his chest looks as though she were rising and falling with the motion of waves. His two tame toucans, one named Timbuc and the other named Timbuctoo, perch on his shoulders. You really can't see, by this light, the brilliant colors of their feathers, but you can see their great beaks jutting out, almost like guns from the side of a battleship.

The thoughts of Great-Uncle Thomas are tenderly turning toward his relatives, and he remembers other homecomings—the time, long years ago, when the twins, Ella and Bella, were little girls, and he brought them tartan dresses from bonny Scotland, the tulip bulbs he brought from Turkey for Lucy's garden, the tiger he brought Francis and had to take back because Bella was afraid it wouldn't get on with Pussy the cat and Quentin, the teapot with a blue Chinaman on it that she liked better than the tiger (you and I know that teapot), and the big wicker cage of tropical butterflies for Cousin Clement to set free in his conservatory.

"Shiver my timbers!" cries Great-Uncle Thomas. (Please don't ask me what that means. I have heard that it is something sailors say, although I have never heard a sailor say it, have you?)

"I beg your pardon?" says the Terrible Turk, in Turkish. He speaks no English.

"I said shiver my timbers," says Great-Uncle Thomas, in Turkish this time. (I do hope you don't mind my changing it to English.)

"I beg your pardon?" says the Terrible Turk again.

"Don't mention it. I just remembered that my Cousin Clement's birthday is today, unless the hour is later than I think. If so, it was yesterday. Oh, well! We will simply have to have another birthday party for him when we arrive. One isn't ninety-nine years old every day."

He goes on to tell about each member of the family, and how warmly each will welcome the Terrible Turk (who is rather timid) and the Smiling Sultan (who is rather shy) and, of course, Great-Uncle Thomas himself.

"I can see them now!" cries Great-Uncle Thomas (Timbuc, Timbuctoo, and the Terrible Turk lean forward and gaze anxiously at the horizon, to see whether they can see them, too.) "All safe and happy in their peaceful homes, never dreaming that we are on our way to visit them. Yes, I can see them now!"

We can see them now—or we can see all of them except Cousin Clement and Apple—and people less safe, less happy, and less at home have seldom been seen.

Yet now, as their new friend leaps upon them, wagging his tail, hope wakes in their hearts.

"Whose little dog are you?" asks Mr. Perkins, who has been missing his poodle, his Pekingese, his Pomeranian, and all the puppies. "What's your name, sir? Tell me, now! Tell me!"

Yet I think he would have been surprised if the little dog had answered, "I am Deerfoot the Indian's dog, and my name is Sir Droppit."

"My advice is, follow him," Mr. Roberts advises. "We are getting nowhere, and he may lead us somewhere."

Sir Droppit is delighted to lead them. He leads them straight to where Deerfoot, Gumbo, and old medicine man from the mountains Mud-on-His-Moccasins are still snoring.

"Don't wake them suddenly," Mr. Roberts advises Uncle Francis, who is about to shake the sleeping redskins. "Indians often scalp you if you wake them suddenly. I speak as one who knows. I will give the call of the thrush and they will think it is morning, and wake."

So Mr. Roberts gives the call of the thrush.

"Uoli-a-e-o-li-noli-nol-aeolee-lee!"

No, he isn't making this up. It is printed right there in his bird book, and in a bird book that I have, too.

And the Indians do wake, and think it is morning.

Gumbo grunts and rolls over, to try to go to sleep again.

Deerfoot begins to do his exercises, touching his toes twenty times without bending his knees.

⟶ *These are the Twins, Ella and Bella, a long time ago, in the Tartan dresses Great-Uncle Thomas brought them from Bonny Scotland. Bella's is still tidy, but Ella has a tear in hers. He brought them the toy Train and the toy tiger, too. Ella is touching and tasting the Tokay grapes and tangerines on the tea table, that holds tarts, too, and teakettle, Teapot, and Teacups. Toby, their terrier, watches them, and so do a Turtle and a tree toad. A toad is looking at some Toadstools under a tree where a thrush is trilling. The butterflies around the tulips are Tortoiseshell and two-spots. Not a glimpse of a Zebra butterfly yet!*

But Medicine Man Mud-on-His-Moccasins is more old-fashioned, and, besides, is waked from a dream of his younger days, so that he springs to his feet and scalps the nearest paleface, who happens to be Cousin Kate.

He wouldn't have done it if he hadn't been half asleep, and he is ashamed, and hangs his head.

But the cries of Gumbo and Deerfoot make him look up.

The red wool wig is in his hand, yet there is a fine head of orange hair on the scalped paleface squaw.

Mud-on-His-Moccasins is good at magic, but he couldn't have done that.

He begins to dance around her, head down, arms flapping, singing a song in Indian that means, "Please excuse me for scalping you, and please don't work bad magic on me—see, I am as helpless as a little bird with broken wings. Please don't turn me into a mouse or a melon seed. Let me, oh Best Magician, remain Mud-on-His-Moccasins, Second-Best Magician, and I'll do anything you say!"

Deerfoot and Gumbo join the dance and the song, and Cousin Kate, who hasn't enjoyed herself as much in years, sings, too. She doesn't know any real Indian songs, but, to be polite, she sings as much as she can remember of "Pretty Redwing," a song about an Indian maiden, filling in with the call of the thrush, or of Mr. Roberts.

> *Oh, the moon shines tonight on pretty Redwing,*
> *Uoli beaming,*
> *The campfires gleaming,*
> *Oh, the moon shines bright on pretty Redwing,*
> *A-e-o-li-lee,*
> *Uoli-a!*

You and I know the noise that she can make when she sings, but it is new to the red men, who shake in their moccasins at such mighty magic, and give her their tomahawks, their eagle feathers, and some fine examples of Indian beadwork.

Then she gives what is left of the wool wig to Mud-on-His-Moc-

126

casins, Uncle Francis gives his necktie (rather old, but a fine bright green for St. Patrick's Day) to Gumbo, who ties it around his scalp lock, and Mr. Roberts gives the rose-geranium soap to Deerfoot, saying in a loud, clear voice, "Best—soap."

Deerfoot takes a small bite and looks amazed. But he does not want to be less polite than the pale- (but not very pale) face chief in the lace war bonnet (that is Mr. Roberts with Cousin Lucy's lace scarf binding the raspberry juice). So he seeks advice from Mr. Perkins. Deerfoot feels more at home with Mr. Perkins than with the others, since he thinks Mr. Perkins is a squaw—a strange-looking squaw, with a mustache, but certainly a squaw, because of the papoose (Jocko in the postbag) on his back.

"Soap good to eat?" he whispers.

"Delicious!" says hungry Mr. Perkins, who thinks Deerfoot has said soup.

Deerfoot tries again, doesn't like it any better, and, foaming lightly at the mouth with soapsuds, hides what is left under his leather waistcoat, thinking that he would rather eat berries and edible roots for the rest of his life than try another nibble of delicious soap.

Now Uncle Francis asks, "Excuse me, gentlemen, but have you seen anything that looks as if it might possibly be a little lost boy in the woods?"

Mud-on-His-Moccasins shakes his head.

Gumbo shakes his head.

Deerfoot nods until he nearly breaks his neck.

"With—old—man?" Uncle Francis asks.

"Yes! Yes!" Deerfoot answers, nodding even harder, for he certainly is with an old man. He is with his grandfather, Mud-on-His-Moccasins, who is often called by family and friends Old-Man-Many-Moons, an Indian way of saying very old indeed.

"Then Apple is with Cousin Clement!" Uncle Francis cries, and the searchers cheer and clap, for now they are sure that Apple is safe.

No telling when Cousin Clement will bring him home, but bring Apple home safely he certainly will.

Deerfoot is so pleased at having given an answer that pleases them that he dances another dance (called the Dance of the Joyful Cottontail Rabbit) all by himself, and then offers to lead them home by a pretty short cut.

Clasping each other's wrists, he and Gumbo make a chair to carry Cousin Kate Lady-to-London at the head of the procession.

Cousin Kate is decked in Indian beadwork, and wears the eagle feathers in her hair (her own hair, at which Mud-on-His-Moccasins keeps stealing bewildered and frightened glances), and, I must admit, she is showing off, bowing and smiling from on high and saying kindly, "Follow me!"

Then, only pausing once to express surprise at the seventh clue, the new brook plowed by Elephant, that makes Uncle Francis think longingly of his fishing tackle, Deerfoot and Gumbo and Sir Droppit the dog lead our party on.

U

"Lead on, oh Chief and Chief and Chief!"
Cries Uncle Francis then.
"All three of you, to my belief,
Bravest and best of men!"

So Deerfoot and Gumbo, hanging their heads to show modesty, but unable to hide their pleased smiles at being addressed as Chief and Chief, lead on, and so does Mud-on-His-Moccasins, still too bewildered by the wool wig to notice what anyone calls him.

They are well along when Uncle Francis remembers that he has left his umbrella on the branch of an umbrageous (I needn't tell you that means shady, for I'm sure you use that word as often as I do— yes, I *am* sure; how many times have you used it? Well, neither have I, *ever*) tree, and they all go back, and then start over again.

How fortunate that Uncle Francis remembered! For one of the party is traveling in his umbrella, unknown to the others. Who do you think?

I will give you three guesses and three hints.

First Hint—She is small and silvery.

Second Hint—We last saw her in a hat, but not wearing it on her head.

Third Hint—She is a swimmer.

Yes! Common Silverside. When Uncle Francis and Aunt Bella were making preparations for the search, one or the other hit against

Uncle Francis' hat, that was on the table against which his half-open umbrella was leaning, and the water and Common Silverside spilled into the umbrella.

As dew has continually fallen into it from the bushes and trees Uncle Francis pushed past, the little fish is feeling perfectly well again in the dew pool, but she is anxious about Apple.

She is the only one who is anxious. The others, believing now that he is safe with Cousin Clement, are enjoying laughter and lighthearted chat (all except Quentin; even Jocko is having fun telling an umbrette—a crested wading bird from Africa, it says on her cage when she is at home at the Zoo—what he thinks of her). Cousin Kate tells Uncle Francis that he should hold his umbrella over her, as Great-Uncle Thomas once said that in the Orient an umbrella is the sign of royalty—or perhaps she should have a white one, like the one carried over the King of Siam, umbrella springing from umbrella top, each gold-fringed, each smaller, until it is a seven-layered umbrella. Or one like the umbrella Great-Uncle Thomas saw in Ceylon, made of fresh marigolds.

"To match my hair," says Cousin Kate, for tonight she is thinking of her hair as the color of marigolds, orange marmalade, new pennies, and butterflies, because she is having such fun.

"Kate, why are *you* the only one to be carried?" asks Aunt Ella, who is growing tired of walking and growing even more tired of Cousin Kate's grand airs.

Cousin Kate doesn't know why any more than Aunt Ella does, so that she can only answer, "Why not?"

So on they go, in this order:

Sir Droppit, prancing and wagging his tail.

Gumbo and Deerfoot, carrying Cousin Kate.

Mud-on-His-Moccasins carrying the red wool wig as though he expected it to bite him.

Aunt Bella leaning on the arm of Uncle Francis, and Common Silverside (unknown to the others) riding in his umbrella.

Cousin Lucy leaning on the arm of Mr. Roberts, who seems to have entirely recovered from his accident, although he still wears the raspberry-soaked lace scarf.

Aunt Ella, who tried to lean on the arm of Mr. Perkins, but who finds him now leaning on her, as he is the most tired of them all, since before this long night's walk he spent a long day walking, delivering letters. And, in Mr. Perkins' postbag, Jocko, who is now taking another nap.

And, far far far behind them all,

Quentin.

Let us leave these friends in charge of their guides, and see what is happening to our friend Apple.

The last time we saw him, Apple, with Caterpillar on his shoulder, had fallen from a tree onto Elephant's back. Elephant had thought Apple was the mouse who had terrified him (nobody, not even himself, thinks anything about sleeping Caterpillar), and the three of them were going lickety-split through the woods.

That is what they are doing yet.

Elephant rockets on, and Apple bounces like a grasshopper all over his back, and would have fallen off if Elephant's back had not been so broad. Now he is sitting at Elephant's tail, facing backward, now he lands face down across Elephant's back, feeling unhappy, and looking like a wet bathing suit spread out to dry. Now he manages to grasp an edge of Elephant's ear and hold on.

Elephant plunges through great lengths of wild grapevine that cover him and Apple with a green net rustling with leaves and heavy with bunches of green grapes that spill and fly like beads from broken strings. Then branches catch the vine net and drag it off, and Apple is able to observe his fellow passengers, those that fall off branches set swaying by Elephant as though he were a wave of the sea washing through the woods, and those bolder ones that jump down for the fun of the ride. Some are wood creatures, some are from the Zoo. At one moment Apple shares Elephant's back with an owl, a flying squirrel, an umbrella bird—like a black crow with a red feather bib and a blue feather pompadour that some people think is like an umbrella, although I don't see why—an empty nest, a unau (you know!) with her baby holding onto her back, and an unga-puti holding onto her baby in front.

The unau, or sloth, is one of the slowest creatures in the world, and the unga-puti, or agile gibbon (another of Jocko's cousins), is one of the swiftest, but they get off together at the next low branch, the unga-puti shooting off like a shooting star, the unau just managing to lift a

132

Aunt Bella hangs upon one of Uncle Francis' arms, and his ulster and umbrella hang upon the other. An umbrette behind them is trying to be useful by picking up Aunt Bella's hairpins. They are unaware of him, and of the Unga-puti and her baby and the Unau and her baby watching from up in the tree, and of an unseen friend traveling in the umbrella.

slow paw in time, and letting herself and her baby be pulled like a bag of wet sand.

The next moment Apple is alone on the broad gray back, holding to Elephant's ear, while branches comb his hair and the tropical birds that cling to them are set screaming and rocking.

No, not alone. Through the wild night ride, sleeping Caterpillar rides with him, unseen and unfelt, lashed to his shoulder by strong silk threads.

It is a long runaway before Elephant decides that the woods are safe, not a creature in them except jaguars, bluejays, lions, rabbits, and boa constrictors looped like ropes from the branches. Not a mouse anywhere. He slows to a tired amble, and he and Apple and Caterpillar come to a beautiful and peaceful place.

The moon, growing pale and sliding down the sky, shines on a sheet of water like a looking glass, its surface only broken by one wet gray rock and one mossy old log, at a narrow place where they make a sort of bridge to the opposite shore, and by hundreds of white water lilies, their petals folded in sleep. Water birds stand, each on one long leg, in the reeds around the shore, their heads still under their wings.

Elephant flops down—quite a flop, as he weighs nine thousand pounds—with a sigh like the wind blowing, and goes to sleep.

Apple slides off him—a slide that feels like a ride down an uncomfortable Shoot-the Chute—flops down on the comfortable bed of tender grass and wild violets—not such a flop as Elephant's, as Apple weighs fifty-seven pounds—with a sigh like a boy sighing, and goes to sleep.

Caterpillar remains on Apple's shoulder. I don't know how much he weighs, but not much. He doesn't sigh, and he is asleep already.

And at that moment, a procession arrives on the other side of the pond.

Sir Droppit, still wagging his tail.

Gumbo and Deerfoot, their knees beginning to bend under the weight of their fair burden (meaning Cousin Kate).

Mud-on-His-Moccasins, carrying the wool wig.

Aunt Bella, and Uncle Francis carrying Common Silverside.

Mr. Roberts, and Cousin Lucy carrying a bunch of pretty wild flowers and a few small insects she hasn't noticed.

Aunt Ella, almost carrying poor tired Mr. Perkins, who is carrying Jocko in the postbag.

Quentin isn't in sight yet, but he is on his way.

The palefaces are to wait here, while the redskins go for their canoes, to make the rest of the journey by water.

"My advice is that we wait on yon far shore," Mr. Roberts advises. "See, it is moon-set and soon will be time for breakfast, and methinks I descry wild strawberries across the lake—"

"He means he thinks he sees them," Aunt Ella explains to Mr. Perkins.

"—and a large rock for these fair ladies to lean against" (Mr. Roberts points to the sleeping Elephant) "while we gentlemen pick their breakfast."

"Don't worry; you can lean and I will pick for us both," Aunt Ella encourages Mr. Perkins.

"And, see," Mr. Roberts goes on, "here is another rock and a log to cross by—first the log, then a little leap to the rock, then just a jump to the violet-cushioned opposite shore."

Aunt Bella,

Uncle Francis,

Cousin Kate,

Aunt Ella,

and Mr. Perkins

cry at the same instant:

"I never could, and Quentin couldn't either!"

"Absolutely crazy!"

"Someone will have to carry me!"

"Stuff and nonsense!" (This cry comes from Aunt Ella, and I wish you would tell me whether she means Mr. Roberts' plan for crossing or Cousin Kate's plan for being carried is stuff and nonsense.)

"Oh, *no!*" (This is poor Mr. Perkins; I mention it for fear you have lost count.)

But Cousin Lucy begs, "Oh, Mr. Roberts, be careful! Think of yourself, and not of resting places and strawberries for us! You are too unselfish and too brave!"

Mr. Roberts bows low, kisses his hand to her, and crying, "Ladies and gentlemen, follow me!" springs to the mossy log.

The gray stone, that is Hippopotamus, goes down, making a swell that rocks the water lilies and sends the frogs diving with cries of "Eek! Eek!" The water birds—the herons, the ibis, the adjutant bird, the umbrette, the pelican, all of whom have gathered here—rise flapping. Deerfoot's ducks, waked from their sleep among the rushes, fly up quacking their danger signal, and circle overhead.

And the mossy log opens tremendous jaws, and the mossy log's tail churns the water (where the rose-geranium soap has fallen from Deerfoot's leather waistcoat) to soapsuds, and from the soap-and-water-filled nostrils of the mossy log float two streams of pretty soap bubbles.

Because, as you and I have known all along, the mossy log on which Mr. Roberts is trying to keep his balance is Crocodile.

V

Crocodile thinks, "Now I shall dine!"
Yet Mr. R. stands straight.
"Oh, Lucy, love, say you'll be mine,
Before it is too late!"

Crocodile really should have thought, "Now I shall breakfast!" But he has been under water for so long, hoping for *some*one to eat, *some*time, that you can't blame him for being confused.

Has that time come at last?

No!

With one graceful leap Mr. Roberts is back where he came from, and has fallen on his knees at Cousin Lucy's feet, repeating, "Oh, Lucy, love, say you'll be mine!"

Cousin Lucy, although at first she is so overcome that she has to sniff the smelling salts in her vinaigrette, whispers, "Yes, Rollo!"

Up comes the sun, turning water and water lilies pink, and making the rose-geranium soapsuds glow with soap-bubble colors. The sun strikes a diamond flash from the stone in the mouth of Quentin, who now waddles out of the woods, to be fondly greeted by Aunt Bella and Sir Droppit. From the opposite bank the fragrance of strawberries floats in a delicate cloud to the noses of our friends, but everyone except Crocodile has forgotten breakfast, and he doesn't care for strawberries.

He now crawls moodily away, really vexed, down the river that flows through a valley into the lake, his way marked by streaming clouds of small soap bubbles sent out by his angry puffing (for his nose is still full of rose-geranium soap and lake water). The bubbles, violet, gold, and green, float up toward the sky, to shine like stars in daylight or sink to bounce gently on the water and break. Then out pour other swirling clouds of them, to delight everyone but Crocodile. They are no comfort to him.

That poor hungry Crocodile—I'm almost beginning to feel sorry for him. Still, it would have been hard on Mr. Roberts to be his breakfast.

Everyone except Crocodile is in highest spirits. Deerfoot and Gumbo, between them, make a very pretty vase from the clay of the lake bank, for Indians are skillful in modeling with clay, and hastily gather and crush roots and berries to make vermilion color to decorate it with pictures of the happy event—forest trees, Mr. Roberts proposing to Cousin Lucy, Setting Moon, and Rising Sun—and the others gather violets to fill it and present it to the blushing couple. The air rings with bird song, and Mr. Roberts, after a peep into his bird book, is able to tell the rest that their feathered friends are vireos.

Then, while the Indians and Sir Droppit go for canoes, the others make plans for the wedding, all except Mr. Roberts, who is telling Cousin Lucy that she is like the bright star Venus, and Cousin Lucy, who is asking Mr. Roberts if it was he who sent her a beautiful Valentine on last Saint Valentine's Day.

"Let us have vanilla ice-cream cones for refreshments," suggests Uncle Francis. "And no vegetables!"

"Plenty of violins," says Cousin Kate. "What is a valse without violins?"

"What is a valse *with* violins?" Mr. Perkins whispers to Aunt Ella.

"A valse is a waltz. Kate is just showing us that she can speak French."

"Vell, vell! Vonderful!" says Mr. Perkins.

"Hip! Hip!" cries Uncle Francis, and they all join in "Hooray!" as five birch-bark canoes sweep into sight, containing not only Deer-

Gumbo and Deerfoot make a Vase. Sir Droppit tries in vain to help, and a vole ventures to peep at them. A vireo flies overhead. The butterflies about the vervain are Vanessas, and the one above the violets is the Viceroy. We seem to be able to find every variety except a Zebra.

Here is a Valse, danced to "Tales from the Vienna Woods" played by a violinist. I never saw Mr. Perkins without his post-bag, and with a vermilion Henry Vaughan carnation in his buttonhole, but I think this is Mr. Perkins. And I never saw Cousin Kate when she wasn't singing, but who else would be wearing a wool wig with a wool nest holding a veery made of velvet? Probably this is just a vision Cousin Kate is having in her mind. The ballroom wall is painted with a view of Venice.

foot, Gumbo, Mud-on-His-Moccasins, and Sir Droppit, but Deerfoot's Squaw Pinkfeather with Fawnfoot the papoose on her back, her mother Squaw Prickly Pear, Deerfoot's mother Squaw Cooing Dove, and a little Indian boy who has come for the ride.

The canoes are decorated with garlands of pine boughs, vines, and bright wild flowers, blue veronica, white verbena, purple vetch, yellow velvet-leaf, and the foamy white blossoms of the viburnum, or do you prefer to call it squaw bush? Or snowball tree, or dog rowan, whitten wood, gaiter tree, cherrywood, red elder, witch hopple, pincushion tree, May rose, cramp bark—oh, you go on, please, if none of these are what you call it. It has quite a good many other names, and Deerfoot and Gumbo use its wood for the shafts of their arrows.

The canoes are named:

Wah-wah-taysee (Little Firefly)

Gitche Gumee

O-mee

O-mi, and

The *B.B.C.* (Birch Bark Canoe) *Victory*.

Deerfoot, Gumbo, and Mud-on-His-Moccasins cannot decide who shall sit in the leading canoe.

Gumbo thinks Big Chief Lace War Bonnet (Mr. Roberts) and the lady who is to be his squaw (Cousin Lucy) should go first.

Mud-on-His-Moccasins thinks Squaw Magic Hair (Cousin Kate) should lead.

But Deerfoot says no; palefaces have a rule for any sort of boat, "Women and children first."

So, still thinking that Mr. Perkins is a squaw and Jocko a papoose, Deerfoot politely hands them into *Wah-wah-taysee* (Little Firefly), signals to Pinkfeather with Fawnfoot to hop in, too, and pushes them off in the lead.

Aunt Ella nearly upsets the canoe, leaping in after them, paying no attention to the distressed cries of Deerfoot, who has other plans for her. Taking the paddle from Mr. Perkins' limp hands, she sweeps ahead, leaving a fine plume of foam, while Pinkfeather strews flowers on the water in honor of the great occasion, and Fawnfoot nearly breaks his neck turning his head to stare at Jocko.

Aunt Ella has never paddled a canoe before, and she hits Mr. Perkins every time she changes the paddle from side to side, but he knows she means it kindly, as indeed she does, so he crouches down and comforts himself with the thought that soon he will be home with his dogs, his parrot, Paddy the donkey, and *no one else.*

"And then I'll never go anywhere ever again," he whispers to himself.

Poor Mr. Perkins! Let's not remind him that when he gets home, *if* he gets home, he will have to start off at once on his day's work of delivering letters. He is having enough trouble without remembering that, as Aunt Ella has now soaked him and herself.

Jocko, who doesn't like getting wet, leaps to Pinkfeather's shoulder, and he and Fawnfoot gaze at each other with equal astonishment.

After *Wah-wah-taysee* (Little Firefly), which is shooting ahead in a zigzag, comes *O-mee*, with Mr. Roberts, Cousin Lucy, Sir Droppit, and Deerfoot, in a race with Gumbo paddling *O-mi*, in which sit Cousin Kate and Cooing Dove (the squaw who won first prize for loudest voice). These two ladies are singing at the same time but not the same song, a sound once heard, never forgotten. Squaw Cooing Dove also throws out handfuls of flowers, and at times beats on a tom-tom she happens to have with her.

Gitche Gumee follows more slowly, full of Uncle Francis (sighing because he hasn't his fishing tackle here) with Common Silverside in his umbrella, Aunt Bella with Quentin, and Mud-on-His-Moccasins.

Last of all comes the *B.B.C. Victory*, bearing Squaw Prickly Pear, who is a large lady, and the little Indian boy, she almost in the water, he so high in air that he cannot reach the river with his paddle, although he tries.

Never did a canoe flotilla proceed with more dash and splash. Bright beads and feathers shine; Cousin Kate's orange hair is as bright as a

The Birch Bark Canoe "Victory," decorated with Virginia creeper with dark berries, Viburnum, with berries, too, lilac Valerian, blue Veronica, and other wild vegetation. Squaw Prickly Pear is paddling, and the little Indian boy is trying to paddle. One of Crocodile's bubbles has burst, frightening a Violet-Wing butterfly. The butterfly we want has black and yellow wings.

143

bonfire. She sings, Cooing Dove sings, Quentin and Sir Droppit bark, and screams arise from various canoes bumped into by Aunt Ella, who is paddling with all her might, sometimes straight ahead, sometimes in a circle, and shipping so much water into *Gitche Gumee* that Uncle Francis opens his umbrella for protection.

Out comes the dew, all over him, and *out* slips Common Silverside, unnoticed, into the river.

With a farewell flip of a fin to the friend who has carried her so far, she swims back toward the shore of the meadow where Elephant, Apple, and Caterpillar are still asleep.

No; excuse me, I am wrong. Apple, wakened by distant but deafening singing, runs to the water's edge, catches a glimpse of faraway canoes through weeping-willow trees, and shouts with all his might.

In vain! The tom-toms, songs, shrieks, barking, and gay laughter drown his shouts.

The canoes disappear; the surface of the lake is empty except for dissolving soapsuds, floating wild flowers, water lilies, and frogs cautiously coming back to sit on the lily pads.

He turns sadly away, wondering again whether anyone has missed him yet and what his dear relatives are doing.

But his spirits rise and his mouth waters as he smells a delicious fragrance, and sees the meadow looking as though thousands of diamonds, rubies, emeralds, and pearls have been spilled on it, dewdrops, and dew-wet wild strawberries, the ruby-red ripe ones and the emerald-green ones, and their pearly blossoms, all sparkling in the sun, while over them flutter countless butterflies, and through them comes Elephant, lifting his trunk in a friendly morning greeting, on his way to bathe.

Thoughts come into Apple's head, all together; he thinks:
How good these strawberries will be for breakfast! And
I want to go bathing, too! And
I wish Cousin Clement could see these butterflies! (They are the kind you and I call Tortoise shell, because of their pretty brown and

black and yellow markings, and that Cousin Clement calls by their Latin name, Vanessa.)

But to return to Apple's thoughts. He thinks:

I wish I could find a Zebra butterfly for Cousin Clement! And

I wish I could find Cousin Clement! And

I wish I could find *anyone*!

Then comes a sensible thought, all by itself.

Mustn't go bathing with a full stomach. Bath first, breakfast afterward.

So he takes off his clothes.

What is this on his coat?

"Hello! A cocoon!" he says.

Can it be the cocoon of the caterpillar he found on his shoulder, when they were up a tree together, that made him feel less lonely?

"I believe it is!" he says, and spreads his coat on the grass, careful not to break the silk threads of the cocoon.

He goes into the water, hugging himself and stepping high at first, as the chill creeps up, then flinging himself in with an enormous SPLASH, and then it is so much fun that he has to jump high and go under, over and over again, shouting for no reason except that he is too happy to keep still.

Elephant gives him a shower bath from his trunk, and Apple splashes as much of Elephant as possible. Then Apple swims, while Common Silverside swims around and around him, overjoyed to see her hero safe, and so much admiring his unusual way of swimming (hopping along with one foot on the bottom) that she tries to do it, too, with the tip of her tail, without much success, while she pours out her adventures—the chase up and down the stream in her effort to save him from Crocodile, finding herself in a tiny pool (Uncle Francis' hat) and then in a deep, dark pool (Uncle Francis' umbrella) that was sometimes still and sometimes stormy, and then—and then—

Apple only sees strings of tiny bubbles rising from her mouth, but she thinks he understands every word, and is happy.

When he floats on his back and looks up at the deep blue sky, Apple is happy, too. When he turns over and looks down through clear water at the wavering light and shadow on the bottom, and the friendly little fish, he is happy. And when, suddenly, he finds that without noticing it he has, for the first time in his life, been swimming without a foot on the bottom, he is so astonished and happy that he nearly bursts.

He tries to show off to Common Silverside, but she thinks his other way of swimming is much more wonderful.

He tries to show off to Elephant, but Elephant is in the meadow now, pulling up tufts of grass for breakfast.

Breakfast!

Out comes Apple, beginning his breakfast with some watercress that grows where the river flows into the lake.

His ears are full of water, and roaring like seashells. So he hops on one foot—pop!—and the other—pop! What a lovely feeling! Now he hears clearly:

the song of the vireos,

the sound of Elephant tearing and munching,

the soft rushing of the river rapids,

the straying sound of a distant cowbell, and

the buzzing of bees around the tall spikes of blue vervain (a wild flower that usually has a cloud of bees around it, and that was supposed, in olden days, to cure sore eyes, make people love you, and keep away witches; I have never tried it for any of these things, but that's what they used to say).

Letting the sun be his towel, Apple gathers his breakfast and eats until he can't hold one strawberry more.

Elephant eats until he can't hold one grass blade more.

"Whooo!" they say, or sigh, together, and bow to one another, each thinking, "Thank you for bringing me to such a pleasant place."

Oh!

Do you see what I see?

A little furry brown and gray creature, with bright eyes and whisking tail, having her breakfast, too, in the tangle of leaves and grasses?

She is a vole or meadow mouse.

If Elephant sees her, get out of his way, or we might as well be sitting on a volcano.

He hasn't seen her yet, and neither has Apple. *She* doesn't care whether they do or not. She is finishing her meal with a little bark from the bottom of the trunk of a viburnum, or squaw bush or witch hopple or gaiter tree—

No! I can't and won't go through all that again, and if you think, "Nobody asked you to," you are right.

Apple puts on his clothes, again careful of the cocoon. Elephant kneels, Apple climbs aboard.

"Home, please, Elephant," he says, trying to sound like Cousin Clement speaking to Caleb, and flicking Elephant lightly with a stalk of blue vervain (a wild flower that usually has a cloud of bees—)

Oh! There I go again! I said all that before. Please excuse me. The trouble is, my mind is taken up with hoping that Elephant doesn't see the little vole.

Slow pitch, slow pitch, like a heavy ship in a slowly heaving sea, Elephant rises (and, of course, Apple rises, and Caterpillar in his cocoon rises), and slowly off they go, away from the vole.

What a relief!

Do you still know where we are?

I don't; I am as lost as Apple is, but I do know that *if* Deerfoot and Gumbo and the others are taking Aunt Bella, Aunt Ella, and the others toward home in *Wah-wah-taysee* (Little Firefly), the *B.B.C. Victory*, and the other canoes, Elephant is taking Apple away from home with every step.

W

Come! Shine your shoes and brush your hair,
Oh, hurry! Don't delay!
And let us greet the happy pair
Upon their Wedding Day.

Aunt Bella wants to wait for the wedding until the wanderers (Cousin Clement and Apple) make their way home. But, as Mr. Roberts says, that may not be for weeks.

"And weeks," adds Cousin Lucy.

"And weeks," says Cousin Kate.

"And weeks," says Uncle Francis.

"And weeks and weeks and weeks and weeks and weeks," says Aunt Ella. "You know Cousin Clement when he is after butterflies."

Yes, Aunt Bella knows Cousin Clement when he is after butterflies, and, indeed, when he isn't.

So the wedding is on Wednesday, just giving time for Aunt Bella and Aunt Ella to bake a wonderful wedding cake, with white-icing orange blossoms. Aunt Ella thinks they might use the still uncut birthday cakes, by putting wreaths of white flowers around them, but Aunt Bella says that would never do.

Cousin Kate makes a white wig trimmed with wool doves with wings cut from paper, to wear when she warbles the Wedding March from *Lohengrin* (by a gentleman named Wagner).

Fortunately, Mr. Roberts' raspberry-juice wounds have disap-

148

peared. As everyone says, you would never guess that he had been scalped.

"Washing my wounds helped wonderfully," he says.

Uncle Willie and Aunt Winifred come from far away, waving warmly, with their little daughters Winona and Wilhelmina, who are to be flower girls.

The Indians come from their wigwams with wedding gifts. The ladies, Cooing Dove, Prickly Pear, and Pinkfeather, bring *Wah-wah-taysee* (Little Firefly) full of water lilies that, when you look closely, are full of water bugs, from the water under the weeping willows, with their good wishes, to remind Cousin Lucy of the wonderful moment when Mr. Roberts escaped from Crocodile. Grandfather Mud-on-His-Moccasins wanted to catch and stuff Crocodile for a wedding present, but could not find him, and has to be content with giving a wild turkey-feather whiskbroom.

Deerfoot and Gumbo have on their best war bonnets that have not been worn for so long that the wings of the moths that fly out make a shimmering cloud. They should have been put away in camphor. (The war bonnets, I mean.)

The bride and groom receive many beautiful presents, but none they appreciate more than a gross of homemade clay vases from Deerfoot and Gumbo.

Mr. and Mrs. Noddy get new white gloves to wear. Of course they get mixed up—Mr. and Mrs. Noddy do, not the gloves. You know those Noddys! They think Cousin Kate is the bride. But no one minds that except Cousin Kate and Mr. Roberts.

Uncle Francis ties white nosegays with white ribbons on the cages of canary Bob and Cockatoo, and around the necks of Pussy the cat, Quentin, Nanny the goat (who eats hers at once), Cousin Kate's kitten, and Sir Droppit, who has come early. Mr. Perkins, arriving with more parcel-post wedding presents, thinks this such a good idea that he puts daisies in Paddy the donkey's panniers, ties bunches of daisies to Polly the parrot's perch, to the collars of his poodle, his Pomeranian, and his

Pekingese, and one to the tail of each puppy (as the puppies are too young for collars yet) and a big bunch to Jocko's tail, as well as a wreath around his neck and another around his red cap. Jocko is also wearing the tiny blue bracelet of Indian beads the searching party found in the woods. Don't ask me how he got hold of that. I really don't know.

"I wish Apple was here," Aunt Bella sighs. "There should be a little page to hold up the bride's train."

"Yes, there should," Aunt Ella agrees. "I don't suppose Fawnfoot the papoose can walk yet, but couldn't Pinkfeather walk backward so that Fawnfoot could lean out of his papoose bag and hold Lucy's train?"

"Or Jocko could be page," suggests Mr. Perkins, looking proudly at Jocko, almost covered with daisies. "Stop scratching, Jocko!"

But Cousin Lucy says that unless Cousin Clement brings Apple back in time, she will have no page.

Alas! Apple is not back in time, and Caleb, who has hitched Hotspur the horse to a wagon and brought it full of watermelons to add to the refreshments, says there has been no word from Cousin Clement.

"How I wish they were here!" Aunt Bella wishes, planning to save large slices of wedding cake for them, each with a whole nosegay of white-icing orange blossoms.

"And how I wish Great-Uncle Thomas was here, instead of being on the other side of the world," says Aunt Ella, who, of course, doesn't know what you and I know about Great-Uncle Thomas' whereabouts. "Think of the wedding presents *he* would give!"

"Oh, Ella! That sounds greedy. I wish I could see Great-Uncle Thomas without a single present."

⟶ *Here is a wasp. It is eating the icing on the wedding cake of Cousin Lucy and Mr. Roberts. The flower girls, holding water lilies, are Winona and Wilhelmina, and their parents, Uncle Willie and Aunt Winifred, watch how wonderfully well-behaved their little daughters are being. Cousin Kate, in a wig made of wire and white wool, is warbling a wedding march, and Mud-On-His-Moccasins, waving his wedding present, a wild turkey-feather whiskbroom, joins with well-meaning war whoops. He has borrowed an old War bonnet to wear to the wedding; those wings behind him are the moths flying out.*

150

"I wish I could, too, Bella. But, as long as we're wishing, why not wish for him *and* presents?"

When the wedding is over the bells ring and the wrens sing, and so do flocks of warblers, accompanied by the drumming of a woodpecker, and all the dogs leap and wag their tails until the bride's path is strewn with fallen-off daisies, and everyone kisses everyone and then eats cake and vanilla ice cream and orange water-ice and watermelon, except Nanny the goat, who kisses no one and eats most of the wide watered-silk sash of one of the flower girls (Winona, I think).

I don't know where all the animals from the Zoo are. The only wild animal present, except for wasps eating cake icing and worrying the guests who want to eat it, too, and a walking-stick insect who has just walked up Mrs. Noddy and made her jump, is a wanderoo (a large black monkey with a white mane, another distant cousin of Jocko's) on the wisteria-covered wall. Jocko starts several times with cakes and chocolates for Cousin Wanderoo, who is too timid to come down and mingle with the other guests, but absent-mindedly eats everything himself on the way, each time.

Now, after photographs are taken of the bride and groom, the orchestra strikes up a waltz.

"I once knew a young lady who waltzed so smoothly that she could hold a glass of water on her head and never spill a drop," says Uncle Francis. "But I can't remember who she was."

"You can't?" cries Aunt Bella and, putting a glass of water on her head, she catches up her skirts and waltzes. (As we learned long ago, Aunt Bella, Aunt Ella and Cousin Kate were called the Three Graces in their youth.)

———➔ *Winona and Wilhelmina drop their white gloves and water liles and climb the wisteria on the wall with wedding cake and watermelon for the welcoming Wanderoo. Wrens sing, butterflies fly (the big butterfly is a Woodnymph and the small one is a Whirlabout, and I will try not to worry any more about seeing no Zebra butterflies) and a walking-stick insect is climbing the wall, too.*

The orchestra breaks into "Over the Waves," everyone cheers, and Aunt Bella turns pink with pleasure. It is only when Uncle Willie, carried away by the beauty of the scene, pursues her with bows and compliments, and then, putting his arm around her waist (or as far around as it will go), joins the dance that the glass of water spills over them both, and the musicians have to change to "April Showers."

Now Caleb, with a white carnation in his buttonhole, and Hotspur, with white ribbons on his harness, come with the calash to take the bride and groom to the station, to begin their wedding trip around the world and to Washington, and everyone waves and shouts good wishes.

With Cousin Lucy and Mr. Roberts gone, and Cousin Clement and Apple not yet returned, and the gentlemen of the orchestra packing their instruments, it seems lonely with no one there except Aunt Bella, Uncle Francis, and, of course, Quentin, Pussy, Cockatoo, the chickens and guinea fowls that have wandered over, Bob the birdie dear, Nanny (although she has disappeared for the moment), Aunt Ella, Cousin Kate and her kitten, Jocko and his cousin Wanderoo, Mr. Perkins and his pets, Mr. and Mrs. Noddy, Uncle Willie, Aunt Winifred and the little flower girls, who are staying for a visit, Deerfoot, Sir Droppit, Gumbo, Pinkfeather and Fawnfoot, Prickly Pear and Cooing Dove.

Mud-on-His-Moccasins, like Nanny, has disappeared, but is soon found asleep behind a flowering weigela bush whose rosy branches are full of wings (attached to bees, hummingbirds, those wasps, hornets, gnats, mosquitoes, butterflies, and such creatures).

They wake him carefully, for everyone is a little tired from the excitement of the wedding and not in the mood to be scalped at the moment.

Now even the redskins must go. They are given more wedding cake and candies in little pleated paper hats, and Squaw Cooing Dove puts *Wah-wah-taysee* (Little Firefly) on her head to take home, and takes it, although Cousin Kate and Aunt Ella, who thought it was a wedding present, try their best to keep it.

154

The weary flower girls, their wreaths wilted and awry, their dresses wrecks from climbing up the wall (for they at last took some goodies to poor patient Wanderoo), and most of Winona's—or *is* it Wilhelmina's—sash inside of Nanny, are sent to bed.

Now it seems even lonelier, and Aunt Bella can't help weeping as she looks wistfully toward the west (which, I do know, happens to be the wrong way) wondering where in the wide, wide world the wanderers (Cousin Clement and Appleby) are, and when they will come home.

X

When the party is ended
And guests say good-by,
Sometimes it seems splendid,
But sometimes you cry.

Mr. Perkins has to go to deliver the late-afternoon mail, and Jocko goes with him.

Cousin Kate rushes into the house to play her new xylophone, a parting present from Cousin Lucy and Mr. Roberts, with a card that said, "Lots of love" and x x x for kisses. Have you a xylophone? I had one once, and could even play "The Bluebells of Scotland" on it, very slowly and a little wrong, but I lost one of the mallets for hitting the notes, and my puppy, Mr. Bumps, chewed the other to pieces.

Mr. and Mrs. Noddy begin to say, "Thank you very much for a lovely time," which, of course, means that they are about to go home,

Cousin Lucy plays her xylophone. The butterfly is a Xerxes—no relation, as far as I know, to Mr. Xerxes Xiros, the photographer. Why couldn't it be a Zebra butterfly? I am getting discouraged about finding one; are you?

but Aunt Bella looks so sad because the party is ending that, to cheer her, they linger, Mr. Noddy pointing out interesting features of the garden to take her mind off her loneliness.

"I see Miss Kate has Xanthoria parietina," he says.

"She *has*?" cries Aunt Bella, and can't keep back a loud sob. "Oh, poor, poor Kate! To lose the company of her dear sister Lucy is bad enough, but now to have—what you said! Oh, oh, oh! Send for the doctor! Poor, unhappy Kate!"

Through the open windows comes the sound of Cousin Kate playing "Yankee Doodle" on her xylophone, at top speed, with lots of extra trills, sounding cheerful indeed, but Aunt Bella continues to sob with pity.

"Dear lady, be calm!" begs Mr. Noddy. "Xanthoria parietina is this yellow lichen on the garden wall."

"Oh!"

"It is a cure for jaundice, an illness that makes your skin yellow."

Aunt Bella looks anxiously at her hands, then at all the faces. The tip of Mr. Noddy's own nose is yellow, but that is yellow with pollen from a lily he had been smelling. Wilhelmina's chin is yellow, because Winona is holding a buttercup under it to see whether her sister likes butter.

Then Mr. Noddy wipes his nose, and Winona drops the buttercup, and no one is yellow at all.

"I don't think any of us has jaundice," Aunt Bella says.

"Oh! And with such a good cure right here! Too bad."

A song floats from a tree full of white, red-flecked flowers, where a beautiful yellow-headed blackbird perches, and Aunt Bella wipes her tears and smiles.

"Oh, listen to the black and yellow bird singing in the Chinese chestnut tree!"

"I beg your pardon? Oh! You mean the Xanthocephalus xanthocephalus—" (this isn't a mistake; if Mr. Noddy says *that name* at all,

157

he should say it twice, although to me it sounds as silly as saying Robert Robert or Sylvia Sylvia) "—singing in the Xanthocares tree?"

If you think Mr. Noddy is showing off, you are right; he is.

"Oh, Mr. Noddy, how *do* you know so much?" exclaims Aunt Winifred.

"Mr. Noddy has been learning Volume X of the Encyclopedia by heart," says Mrs. Noddy, proudly.

Now everything is forgotten in a new excitement; Mr. Xerxes Xiros, the photographer, appears at the garden gate with the photographs of the bride and groom, that he has just developed.

Mr. Xiros is a gentleman from a faraway country. He does not understand English very well, and is rather nervous, so what do you think he did by mistake?

He took X-ray photographs instead of ordinary ones.

As you know, an X-ray photograph shows the pennies in your pocket (if you are lucky enough to have any) and the bones in your body. So there are Mr. Roberts and Cousin Lucy and the flower girls and Jocko (who hid under the bride's train and popped out just in time to get into each picture) with every bone showing.

"How unusual!" cries Aunt Winifred.

"How interesting!" says Uncle Francis.

"These I like!" says Aunt Ella. "I had completely forgotten my bones, and I'm delighted to be reminded of them."

"Yes, indeed," Uncle Francis agrees. "What would we be without our bones? Limp as boiled macaroni!"

"Without bones in our fingers, you and I couldn't have made the wedding cake, Bella," says Aunt Ella.

"Without bones in my legs I couldn't go fishing," Uncle Francis says.

"And I couldn't waltz with a glass of water on my head," Aunt Bella says.

"Without bones in my arms I couldn't play 'The Bluebells of Scotland' on my new xylophone," adds Cousin Kate, who has rushed out

158

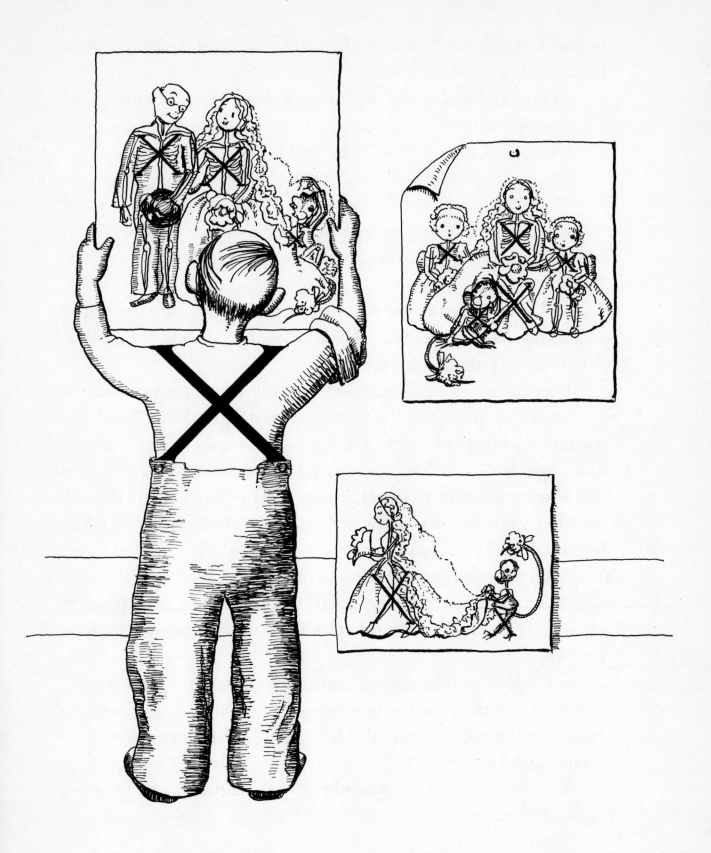

Mr. Xerxes Xiros examines the wedding pictures, and is extremely surprised to find that he has taken X-ray photographs by mistake.

to look at the photographs. "Without my jawbone, I couldn't open my mouth to sing!"

"Three cheers for our dear bones! Hip, Hip, hurrah!" Uncle Francis shouts.

"Also, Ribs, Ribs, hurrah!" Mr. Noddy cries.

"Backbone, Backbone, hurrah!" Aunt Ella adds.

"Tibia, Fibula, hurrah!" roars Uncle Willie, astonishing everyone. "Those are just bones in our legs. We each have two hundred and six bones—do you want me to go on with the other two hundred and four? I can!"

And if you think Uncle Willie is showing off, you are right again.

"Willie has been reading a book called *The Human Body*," Aunt Winifred says proudly. "He can!"

They thank him very much, but say that he must not tire himself.

Then they all engage the surprised and delighted Mr. Xiros, who has been having a bad attack of X-leg (which means knock-knees; his knees have been knocking together for fear the ladies and gentlemen will be cross about the pictures), to take X-ray photographs of them all.

"For we must never again forget how blessed we are in having bones," Uncle Francis says.

"And there is something else we mustn't forget," Aunt Bella says to him and Aunt Ella. "I'm not exactly worried about Cousin Clement. He is experienced in taking care of himself. But we mustn't forget to find Apple.

So Uncle Francis writes on his engagement calendar, "Find Apple," and Aunt Ella ties a loop of blue wool she is knitting into a jacket for Jocko (his red one is getting shabby) around her finger to remind her to find Apple.

Aunt Bella doesn't need anything to remind her, for she misses Apple all the time.

Y

No one can ever quite foresee
When up the sun is rising
Exactly what the day will be.
Sometimes it is surprising.

When the sun rises the day after the wedding, Cousin Kate gets up and goes to the window, happily saying, "Not a thing to do all day but play 'Yankee Doodle' on my new xyl—"

Then, instead of "—ophone," she lets out a yell of surprise, for there, sitting on the dewy grass, are all the Indians.

They had such a good time yesterday that they have come again, bringing also the little Indian boy who sat high in the canoe where Squaw Prickly Pear sat low. The canoe is the *B.B.C. Victory*. I'm sorry that I don't know the little boy's name.

They take Cousin Kate's yell for a greeting, and Cooing Dove answers with an equally loud yell, and the gentlemen give Indian war whoops, just for fun, patting their mouths while they whoop, so that it comes out like the hooting sobs of enormous owls.

"Whoo-whoo-whoo-*WHO-O-O-O!*"

Jocko's distant cousin, the wanderoo, is back also, sitting on the wall, looking timid, but hopeful.

"You wait!" Cousin Kate calls, and slips out the back way and runs to ask Uncle Francis and Aunt Bella (still yearning for Apple) what to do to amuse them.

161

Aunt Ella has also come in to ask advice about amusing Uncle Willie, Aunt Winifred, Winona, and Wilhelmina. She wants to make their visit pleasant, for, after all, they say they can only spend a year.

"What shall we do?" ask Aunt Bella, Aunt Ella, and Cousin Kate, looking at Uncle Francis.

"A picnic. We will have a picnic at the Zoo."

The ladies give three cheers (one apiece) for Uncle Francis' suggestion.

"I will bake a cake," says Aunt Bella.

"All our houses are *full* of cake," says Aunt Ella. "You boil some eggs."

"Then I will make some yeast rolls."

"By the time they are ready, today will be yesterday. Boil some eggs."

So Uncle Francis gathers eggs, and, while Aunt Bella boils them, he catches Nanny the goat and hitches her to her wagon, so that Winona, Wilhelmina, and that little Indian boy can take turns in riding with the freezers of ice cream left from the wedding.

Both birthday cakes and what is left of the wedding cake are packed, and Aunt Bella quickly bakes a fresh cake while no one is looking, just in case there isn't enough. She has no time to decorate it, but, to make up for this, the chocolate icing is twice as thick as the cake part.

She also picks cherries from Cockatoo's tree, where the friendly yellowhammers are peck-peck-pecking at the bark, already having lunch, since they have been up since dawn.

Now they spread their yellow-lined wings for small flights, then back they come. They don't in the least mind Aunt Bella helping herself from their tree.

Our tree, the yellowhammers think; my tree, Cockatoo thinks; our tree, some robins, ants, caterpillars, tree toads, and Uncle Francis and Aunt Bella think.

It seems to be Everyone's Tree.

Aunt Bella would like to take Cockatoo, Bob the canary, and Pussy to the picnic, but Uncle Francis says better not, too many lions and tigers. She does hope Cockatoo, Bob, and Pussy won't notice as she packs a chop bone for Quentin, who, of course, is to be one of the party.

Aunt Ella makes sandwiches and gathers the last of her strawberries.

Caleb hitches Hotspur to the calash, for the ladies who don't care to walk (the wanderoo, although he is no lady, rides on top), and also provides more watermelons.

Mr. and Mrs. Noddy join the party, not quite sure where they are going, and Mr. Xiros is picked up on the way, to take photographs of the happy time.

Mr. Kelly, the kind keeper of the Zoo, welcomes them all, but especially the wanderoo, who is equally glad to see Mr. Kelly, hugs him lovingly, and then goes contentedly to his cage.

A yak who has followed the calash is also warmly welcomed by Mr. Kelly, who is too excited about having even these animals return to pay much attention to Uncle Willie telling how the people in the Himalaya mountains in India, where the yaks come from, use yak butter instead of milk in their tea.

> *"My yak*
> *Has come back,*
> *And my wanderoo,*
> *Too!"*

sings Mr. Kelly, while Mr. and Mrs. Noddy try to make up for his lack of attention by saying, "No!" and "Not really?" in astonished, interested voices to Uncle Willie.

Now a giraffe appears.

"I *did* see that, then!" Caleb mumbles. "I thought I was dreaming."

Now there is an orange flash as a cock-of-the-rock flies into the empty Bird House, followed by a flock of little grass-green parakeets.

Now the paths fill with returning animals and the air fills with returning birds.

Here come the pelicans, here the pink flamingos, their long legs trailing as they fly. PURR, PURR! Here is the lion, purring, not roaring. Here is Cousin Kate's companion of the long night walk, the kangaroo with her baby in her pouch. Here is the python, like yards and yards of garden hose painted brown and yellow, and here are the ibis, the lyrebird, the marabou stork, the koala with her baby on her head. Screaming and streaming, here comes the macaw, brightest blue, shining yellow, and here come the birds of Paradise, with golden backs and silver breasts and long cloudy crimson tails.

Here, among returning leopards and bears and wart hogs, is a small red deer.

"Shoo, shoo, little creature!" Mr. Kelly says gently. "Go back to the woods. Your mother will miss you."

Monkeys hang in garlands and bunches from the trees, by paws and tails, then leap into their cages to swing—*whish!*—on their swings. The seals come barking and clapping their fins. Zebras gallop back (four-footed zebras, not Zebra butterflies, alas!). Here are the agile gibbon (or unga-puti) and her baby, and the sloth (you know, the unau) and her baby, the ones who rode Elephant-back with Apple.

What is this mossy log, with rainbow-colored bubbles drifting above it, crawling along the stream that flows into the tanks in the Zoo gardens, followed by something large and gray like a submarine with a pleasant smile?

Crocodile, of course, hungry, hungry Crocodile, unwillingly blowing a few last soap bubbles, followed by Hippopotamus.

Last, running as fast as she can, comes Ostrich.

Mr. Kelly also runs as fast as he can, to greet and feed each returning friend.

"Hip, Hip, hurrah!" he cries, happy for the first time since the animals ran away.

"Ribs, Ribs, hurrah!" shouts Aunt Ella.

"Humerus, Clavicle, hurrah!" roars Uncle Willie, getting in the names of two more of those two hundred and six bones he knows.

Suddenly Mr. Kelly looks troubled.

"*Some*one is missing," he says. "I can't think which of them—"

Sir Droppit (who, of course, has come with the Indians) begins to bark joyfully, and Quentin quickly hides his chop bone and his bright stone behind Aunt Bella as Mr. Perkins appears with his poodle, his Pomeranian, his Pekingese, and all the puppies, bring post cards that have just come from Cousin Lucy and Mr. Roberts.

The post card for Uncle Francis and Aunt Bella has a picture of a Yeoman of the Guard, and printed under it is "Greetings from London."

The one for Aunt Ella has a Turkish lady in a yashmak (a veil that covers all your face except your eyes) and says, "Greetings from Constantinople."

Uncle Willie's and Aunt Winifred's has a yucca plant in bloom and says "Greetings from New Mexico, Land of Sunshine."

A yoke of white oxen and "Greetings from Italy" is on the card for Winona and Wilhelmina.

Cousin Kate's has a yodeler (if you don't know how to yodel, ask the nearest grown-up to show you, and if he or she says he or she can't, go on asking until you find someone who can and will; it is interesting). This one says "Greetings from Switzerland."

Mr. and Mrs. Noddy's post card has a sprig of yew, and says "Greetings from the Dismal Swamp."

Caleb's has a view of the Yellow River, and says "Greetings from China."

And one for Mr. Perkins has a Yule log and says "Yuletide Greetings."

On each, Cousin Lucy and Mr. Roberts have written, "Having wonderful time. Wish you were here."

(These were all mailed at the station before Cousin Lucy and Mr. Roberts got on the train. They are part of a large post-card collection Mr. Roberts took with him, just in case.)

"We must send them a post card," says Uncle Francis.

Five pennies are quickly collected, and Mr. Kelly (who is still

Here are the post cards Mr. Perkins brought; a lady in a Yashmak, a view of the Yellow River, a Yodeler in the Swiss mountains, a Yucca plant, a Yeoman of the Guard, a sprig of yew, a Yoke of oxen, and a Yule log. A Yellow butterfly has lit on the cards. Yellow is its family name, just as Capple is Appleby's family name. Its special name is Fairy Yellow. I expect this is the last butterfly we'll see. I don't believe any longer that there is such a thing as a Zebra butterfly. Do you?

scratching his head and murmuring, "One of the animals hasn't come back—now *which*?") sells them a picture post card of the Monkey Cage, and they write, "Having wonderful time. Wish you were here."

"Oh, dear! We forgot the stamp. We need another penny," says Aunt Ella.

To everyone's surprise, Caleb gives this penny.

"Mr. Clement would want me to," he says. "And I'll probably get it back with next month's wages—that is, if Mr. Clement ever gets back."

Speaking of the Monkey Cage, as we were before Caleb surprised us, everyone has been too excited to notice a sad-looking Italian gentleman standing before it.

This is Signor Olivetto, who is trying to cheer himself by a look at the monkeys, for he misses Jocko sadly.

Now he begins to play "O Sole Mio" on his hand organ, and—

Out of Mr. Perkins' postbag comes a round red cap, two pricked-up ears, two round bright eyes, and then, with one leap, Jocko is in Signor Olivetto's arms, hugging his old companion and business partner.

We aren't through with surprises yet.

Up sweeps a taxicab, and who do you think get out? And get off? (For two of the newcomers are sitting cross-legged on top to have a better view of the country.)

Who do you guess?

First Mr. Roberts steps out.

Then he helps Cousin Lucy to alight.

Then, bowing in response to the shouts of astonishment and welcome, he explains that just as they were getting on the train, someone got off, so that they got off, too, and came back with—

"Great-Uncle Thomas!"

Out steps Great-Uncle Thomas. Timbuc and Timbuctoo, the toucans, are on his shoulders, and begin to yell at friends they recognize in the big Bird Cage, who yell back at them.

Waving his sailor hat, Great-Uncle Thomas joins in the cheers for himself. Everyone is rejoicing except Caleb, who complains, "Too bad we licked that stamp! Now my good penny is wasted."

Then Great-Uncle Thomas introduces his two friends, who have climbed down from the taxi roof with some trouble, tripping over their long, curved swords and getting tangled in the fringes of their sashes.

The Terrible Turk wears turquoise-blue silk trousers, the twinkling jacket that we saw by moonlight on the deck of the *S.S. Tapioca*, and a towering turban.

The Smiling Sultan is splendid in scarlet silk and silver.

With smiles and bows, he speaks for seven minutes by Uncle Willie's watch, in a language that only he and the Terrible Turk and Great-Uncle Thomas can understand.

"He says he is glad to be here," Great-Uncle Thomas translates, when the Smiling Sultan has finished.

Then the Terrible Turk talks for ten minutes by Uncle Willie's watch, with wider smiles and bows so deep that his turban falls off.

"He says he is, too."

The Terrible Turk gives each lady (including, of course, Winona, Wilhelmina, and Squaws Prickly Pear, Cooing Dove, and Pinkfeather) a tremendous topaz, and the Smiling Sultan gives each of them a sapphire as big as a hen's egg.

Aunt Bella gives the newcomers real hens' eggs, hard-boiled, also sandwiches, strawberries—well, you know, some of everything in the baskets except Quentin's chop bone. The taxi driver says he has never eaten a more delicious lunch in pleasanter company.

Cousin Lucy suddenly screams.

"Oh, Rollo, my dear! What are you doing in the top of that tree? Come down! You will break your neck!"

But Mr. Roberts is on the ground, recalling, with Squaw Cooing Dove, happy hours aboard the *O-mee* and the *O-mi*.

"How pleasant our canoe trip was!" he says.

"How! How!" Cooing Dove replies.

What Cousin Lucy sees among the branches is Chimpanzee, in Mr. Roberts' old silk hat, the one that held the raspberries.

This makes everyone laugh except Mr. Roberts.

"Where is Cousin Clement?" asks Great-Uncle Thomas.

"Here I am, Thomas," replies a well-known voice.

I am just as much surprised by this as anyone is; are you?

Cousin Clement has lost his hat, and a bird could build a nest from the twigs, cobwebs, and other odds and ends in his hair; indeed, a white-throated sparrow is fluttering above him now, with a straw in its beak, probably planning a new home. Cousin Clement's clothes are torn and covered with burrs; his boots are muddy. But he looks well, and greets everyone with pleasure and politeness. He can only tell them that on the way to Aunt Bella's party, he caught just a glimpse of yellow and thought it might be a Zebra butterfly and followed it, he doesn't know where nor for how long.

"And it was a Fairy Yellow instead of the Zebra! How could I have made such a mistake? I must be growing old."

That reminds them to wish him a Happy Birthday, even though their wishes are four days late.

"And here is your birthday cake, with love," says Aunt Bella.

"And here is another, with love," says Aunt Ella.

I never thought Cousin Clement would get those birthday cakes, did you?

Caleb and Hotspur and the calash, and the taxi driver and his taxi, go back to collect Cousin Clement's birthday presents, and Mr. Perkins goes, too, riding in the taxi and enjoying the change from walking, to bring any overflow in the panniers of Paddy the donkey. It is thought better not to send Nanny and the goat wagon (in which Jocko and some other monkeys are now having a ride, or hoping to, if they can ever get Nanny started) for fear that she may eat any presents put in it.

Here are the presents they bring back.

A book on butter-making from Aunt Bella. She hadn't her spectacles on when she bought it, and she thought it was about butterflies.

There are also a quill pen, a plum cake, a bathmat, a nutcracker, and a cherry pie, labeled Happy Birthday to Cousin Clement from Quentin, Pussy, birdie Bob, Nanny goat, and Cockatoo; I suspect Aunt Bella helped with these.

A crown of crimson carnations from Caleb. This is put on top of all the bird's-nest materials in Cousin Clement's hair, and everyone agrees it is wonderfully becoming.

Then Caleb gives Cousin Clement his BIG birthday present.

Perhaps you remember how hard Cousin Clement sometimes tries to win a compliment from Caleb. Not only about his butterfly-painting has Cousin Clement tried, but also when he has a new coat, or eats all his carrots, or plays "The Chimes of Normandy" on his clarinet without any wrong notes.

No success; never a kind word from Caleb.

Now Caleb gives Cousin Clement—

A COMPLIMENT!

"You don't look a day over ninety-nine, sir."

And, as we know, Cousin Clement is four days over ninety-nine.

Cooing Dove tries to persuade Mud-on-His-Moccasins to give her his calumet, or peace pipe, to give to Cousin Clement. It is a very fine one, with carvings of curious creatures and tassels of horsehair, rabbit fur, owl feathers, and eagle feathers, and Mud-on-His-Moccasins values it highly. Shout as she will, he pretends not to hear Cooing Dove, and pull as she will, he won't let go of his calumet.

So that Cooing Dove has to be contented with singing.

She chants something called "The Moon of the Cottontail Rabbit," and Deerfoot does his Joyful Cottontail Rabbit Dance all over again, to her chanting.

Of course, this song and this dance aren't brought back in the calash, the taxicab, or Paddy's panniers, but they are birthday presents, all the same.

Aunt Ella presents Cousin Clement with eleven egg cozies, and an Easter egg made of sugar that looks like snow, with red sugar roses and a white sugar dove on top. When Cousin Clement looks through a tiny window set in a wreath of roses, he sees a little girl holding her muff to her cheek and a little boy in a round cap like one he wore himself ninety-four years ago, skating among snow and roses.

Uncle Francis' gift is a flute.

"Just what we need to prop open the parlor window," Caleb says.

Fawnfoot makes funny faces. That is all that he can do for Cousin Clement's birthday present. It is one of the presents Cousin Clement likes best.

Gumbo, usually glum and gloomy, good-naturedly grunts greetings.

The little Indian boy picked up an ibis feather, and was saving it for a war bonnet when he grows up, but gives it to Cousin Clement instead.

The present Cousin Kate is knitting isn't finished, so she gives Cousin Clement a kind kiss.

Mr. Kelly offers the koala, the kangaroo, and the kinkajou.

Cousin Lucy's gift is a lot of her lovely lilies, and Mr. Roberts' is rhubarb tied with red ribbon.

Caleb grumbles, "We *have* lilies! We *have* rhubarb!"

Medicine Man Mud-on-His-Moccasins surprises everyone by offering (no, not his peace pipe) a fine ear of maize, or Indian corn, with red, black, and orange grains among the yellow.

Signor Olivetto, who has been welcomed into the party by one and all, would have liked to give the onion and the orange he brought for lunch, but he ate the onion and Jocko ate the orange. So he plays "O Sole Mio" on the organ, and Jocko dances a jig, in Cousin Clement's honor, while Mr. Perkins plays prettily on his postman's whistle, and then presents a pound of peppermints.

Prickly Pear and her daughter Pinkfeather want to give something to Cousin Clement.

Saying, "Excuse us, please," they whisper together.

Then they give a play.

Here is the plot of the play.

Prickly Pear is a mother, Pinkfeather is her daughter, and the papoose Fawnfoot is a pumpkin.

Pinkfeather comes to see Prickly Pear, bringing the pumpkin for a present. Prickly Pear makes a pumpkin pie (by rolling pumpkin Fawnfoot into a blanket for pie crust). She and Pinkfeather eat the pie. (Not really; they just kiss the back of the pumpkin's neck, and that tickles him and makes him laugh.) Pinkfeather thanks Prickly Pear for a pleasant time, and they part.

When the applause dies down, the taxi driver tries to toot a tune on the taxicab horn, and the applause springs up again.

Uncle Willie and Aunt Winifred give their warmest wishes, and Winona and Wilhelmina have each painted Cousin Clement a water color, one of a whippoorwill, one of a whale.

The Smiling Sultan and the Terrible Turk are sad and troubled that they did not know they were coming to a birthday party, but the Terrible Turk gives twenty assorted turquoises, tourmalines, and topazes (all he can find in his pockets at the moment, although he knows there are more *some*where), and the Smiling Sultan gives seventy star sapphires.

Mr. Xiros takes an X-ray photograph of Cousin Clement, free.

As for Great-Uncle Thomas, he gives trunkfuls of treasures—tarbooshes (red felt caps with blue silk tassels, and please excuse me if you knew already), tissues woven with tinsel, trumpets, tortoise-shell boxes full of trinkets, tom-toms, a teakwood table, tambourines, turbans, and Turkish Delight; also a tame troupial bird trained to say, "Happy Birthday!"

Timbuc and Timbuctoo the toucans look worried, but Great-Uncle Thomas would never give them away.

"These are just a few trifles for Cousin Clement," Great-Uncle Thomas explains. "Plenty more for all of you when we go home. Keepsakes for one and all, old friends and new."

The Indians give a war whoop and the taxi driver toots his horn, in thanks for Great-Uncle Thomas' thoughtfulness.

Cousin Clement is almost overcome by gratitude for such a birthday party. Not for anything would he tell them that the one thing, the only thing, he really wants for a birthday present is to see a Zebra butterfly.

But he can't help thinking about it, and thinking that he will never see one, and his heart grows heavy.

A dark cloud comes over the sun, and raindrops fall, splashing so hard on the stream that no one notices a little fish putting her head out—Common Silverside, looking for her hero, Apple.

"OH!" shouts Mr. Kelly the keeper. "I've just remembered what I'm missing! *Where is my elephant?*"

And, "OH!" cries Aunt Bella at the same moment. "We all thought he was with Cousin Clement, and he wasn't! *Where is Apple?*"

Z

Oh, many an anxious face I see,
And hear some loud boo-hooing.
Come, quickly come away with me,
Let's find what Apple's doing.

While tears for Appleby's absence wet the cheeks of some, rain wets the clothes of everybody, and only Caleb is happy, as he transplanted his zinnias early this morning, and the rain will make them grow. The beautiful embroidered Zouave jackets of the Smiling Sultan and the Terrible Turk are dark with rain. The only article of clothing that looks fresher for the soaking is Cousin Clement's carnation crown.

173

They all crowd into the Tropical Bird House, that Mr. Kelly has worked hard to make as much like a jungle as possible. He wants his birds to feel at home. From among dark-and-light-green-striped leaves of zebra plants from Brazil and the beautiful white flowers of the Zantedaschia aethiopica from Africa (perhaps you'll thank me to call these by their other name, calla lilies—and I'll thank you if you will), ferns tall as trees rise to the glass roof where the rain spatters and streams.

Caleb, by the way, is calling *those flowers* calla lilies at this moment.

"*We* have calla lilies," he says, and Cousin Clement has to cough politely to keep Mr. Kelly from hearing the rest. "*Our* calla lilies are much finer."

In hanging moss baskets bloom the deep-pink flowers of the—here we go again— Zyocactus (Christmas cactus) from Brazil, too, and the —oh, dear me!—Zygopetalum orchids (rare flowers—fortunately, with that name! Suppose Cousin Kate, instead of singing "My love is like a red, red rose," had to sing "My love is like a striped, striped"— Zyg-and-so-forths are striped like zebras, except that I've never seen a purple-and-white zebra. Where are we? Oh, suppose Cousin Kate had to sing, "My love is like a striped, striped Zygopetalum.")

Will you please tell me how Mr. Noddy ever learned Volume X of the Encyclopedia by heart? I have had to copy each of these Zs—Zantedaschia, Zyocactus, Zygopetalum—from the labels Mr. Kelly has thoughtfully put on the plants, and even now, unless I look again, I can only remember calla lily, Christmas cactus, and orchid.

Or does it seem easy to you?

Mr. Kelly receives many compliments on his Tropical House, although not quite as many as he has hoped for. Great-Uncle Thomas is giving a talk on his exploring trips through South American jungles. Mr. Roberts is trying to learn some tropical bird calls—not easy, as the birds are all shrieking, creaking, and whistling together, while the dove-looking bell bird lets out such yells as must be heard to be believed, so that the only new bird call Mr. Roberts is sure of is "Happy Birthday," that the troupial bird Great-Uncle Thomas brought for Cousin Clement

174

keeps calling. Aunt Ella is telling poor Mr. Kelly, who has worked terribly hard at printing the labels and at getting the spelling right, that he should have marked the plants with simpler names. Aunt Bella is too anxious about Apple to think of the Tropical House or of anything else. And Caleb keeps saying, "*Hmph!* No carnations!"

Kind Cousin Lucy and Mr. and Mrs. Noddy try to make up for this by telling Mr. Kelly how beautiful the Zan-you-know and the Zyo-and-so-on and the Zyg-and-the-rest-of-it are.

They really are, too.

But it is hot in the Tropical House. Everyone's clothes begin to steam slightly. Everyone's face begins to look boiled.

Let's go outside for some air.

Here is Nanny goat, who has eaten some zwieback, all that was left in a picnic basket, and is now eating the basket, not in the least minding the rain that splashes in her little green goat wagon.

I don't mind the rain, either. Do you? Let's run down the road to the woods and try to find Apple.

Wait a minute! Do you hear what I hear?

SWISH—SWISH—

Swishing through the trees, out of the woods comes Elephant, ridden by Apple, who is crouching as the low branches spill icy trickles down his back, and holding his hand over Caterpillar's cocoon, so that his friend won't be swept off his shoulder.

You can see that Elephant knows where he is going now.

He swings toward a roadside restaurant called the Zanzibar cafe, where the musicians of a circus brass band have just finished a big mid-day dinner. They are so full of potatoes and gravy, dumplings and gravy, rice and gravy, bread and gravy, and gravy that they are sleepy, but suddenly a bugler near the window plays "Boots and Saddles" on his bugle, then cries, "Here come the elephants! The parade has started!"

Out they rush, thinking it is their circus parade, buttoning their scarlet, gold-braided tunics, with a good many buttons buttoned into

Drum Major Zachary Zipp leaves the Zanzibar Café. You can see its name on the sign with the Zebra, over the door. He surprises a white-throated sparrow near the zinnias. I needn't remind you that the sparrow's other name is—wait a minute! What is its other name? Oh, yes! Zonotrichia albicollis. It was just on the tip of my tongue, but thank you for reminding me.

wrong buttonholes, for they are still dreamy because of all that gravy, and get into step, after a good deal of hopping and changing feet.

With a roll of drums and a flourish of trumpets, they burst into "The Entrance of the Gladiators" as they, Elephant, Apple, and Caterpillar sweep through the gates of the Zoo.

At the sound of the brass band, out bursts everyone from the Tropical Bird House.

Out bursts the sun, too, and a glorious double rainbow appears in the sky. Mud-on-His-Moccasins is sure that Cousin Kate has made the rainbow appear, to match her hair—she is wearing the old rainbow wig Aunt Bella made for her—and wonders whether he dare ask her to teach him just this one magic.

Apple sees a throng of family, friends, and friendly strangers, all the faces beaming with welcoming smiles.

The sun shines bright on the paint and beads and feathers of the Indians (Deerfoot and Gumbo have actually painted on blue and yellow smiles today, instead of their usual frowns and sneers). It shines on Uncle Francis' Saint Patrick's Day green necktie still around Gumbo's scalp lock, on the glass-bead raindrops in Cousin Kate's rainbow wig, on Jocko's scarlet cap and jacket and blue bead bracelet, on Cousin Clement's crimson carnation crown sparkling with raindrops, on the bright silk and silver of the Terrible Turk and the Smiling Sultan, and on a lot of diamonds, sapphires, emeralds, and rubies that the Smiling Sultan spills when he pulls out his handkerchief to wave, and it strikes a diamond flash from the stone that Quentin is carrying again. (He has buried his chop bone.) It makes Timbuc and Timbuctoo, the toucans, glow like colored glass with light coming through. When we first met them, by moonlight, on the deck of the good, but perhaps not *very* good, ship *Tapioca*, we couldn't see their colors, but look at them now! Their backs and wings and tails are black as blackest, wettest ink, their breasts are crimson, they have orange feather bibs edged with lemon, their claws are blue, their enormous beaks are green, and their round, interested eyes are set in scarlet patches. They are enough to make us

177

blink, in this sunlight that throws rainbows around even the dust-colored *Zonothrichia albicollis*—oh, white-throated sparrows! This is the last long word beginning with Z that I am going to use. You won't mind, will you? And certainly the sparrows won't mind. They are trying to eat the diamonds, emeralds, sapphires, and rubies the Smiling Sultan spilled, and deciding that they are no good. But they don't mind this, either, since they have had so many good picnic breadcrumbs that they aren't hungry. If we had not stayed such a long time in the Tropical House—it was my fault, copying the names of *those flowers*—we would have heard the white-throated sparrows giving thanks for the crumbs, singing sweetly in the rain, as they love to do.

The sun shines on the stream, and on good little Common Silverside leaping in a shower of diamond drops, rejoicing to see her dear friends, Uncle Francis and Apple, safe and together.

The sun shines on the very last soap bubble floating up from Crocodile, safe in his comfortable tank—the last, the loveliest bubble, its deep, bright colors swirling, green, violet, rose, gold, green. Up, up—

Up—

Good-by, soap bubble. Good-by, last trace of Mr. Roberts' rose-geranium soap.

The sun shines on tears of joy pouring down Aunt Bella's face, and Apple wants to run into her arms.

He tries, with pokes and kicks, to make Elephant let him down. But, either because they are signals by accident, or because of pleasure at seeing Mr. Kelly, Elephant goes through every trick he has ever learned.

First he stands on his hind legs with his trunk in the air.

Next he waltzes.

The circus band begins to play. It plays "The Gold and Silver Waltz" so beautifully that everyone bows to everyone and waltzes, too, except Signor Olivetto, who is adding to the music with "O Sole Mio," "The Wearing of the Green," and the tune whose name no one can remember, on the hand organ, Great-Uncle Thomas, who plays on the zummarah, or shepherd's pipe, that he brought from Egypt, Cousin Clement, who surprises everyone by playing trills on his birthday-present flute, and the Smiling Sultan, who is sweeping showers of notes from a zither he hauls out, together with a shower of pearls, dates, red and white ivory chessmen, clean pocket handkerchiefs, his toothbrush, gold pieces, and photographs of far-off loved ones, from those Turkish trousers of his that look like silk laundry bags full of laundry.

And, of course, Cousin Kate plays her xylophone (which you may be sure she has brought) and sings, and Cooing Dove sings, too, and Mr. Roberts, although he is waltzing with Cousin Lucy, gives the call of the thrush—you remember, "Uoli-a-e-o-li-noli-nol-aeolee-lee!"

That reminds Cousin Kate to sing her Indian song, changing it a little, now that she knows the Indian ladies, to be polite to them all.

"Oh, the sun shines today on pretty Cooing Dove,
Prickly Pear, Pinkfeather, and Fawnfoot,
and especially on our dear Appleby,
Uoli beaming,
The bright smiles gleaming,
Oh, the sun shines bright on pretty Cooing Dove,
Prickly Pear, Pinkfeather, and Fawnfoot,
and all the rest of us, but particularly
on our dearest Apple;
A-e-o-li-lee,
Uoli-a!"

Mr. Kelly is busy turning on the Zoo Fountain, which rises to a height of nearly four feet, and catches a rainbow before it topples to one side. Mr. Xiros is running around taking photographs. But everyone else is dancing.

Even the Indians, pad-pad-padding with their moccasined feet, shake gourd rattles, beat tom-toms, and do a war dance (just from fun and excitement, not mad at anyone) to waltz time, and Great-Uncle Thomas, still playing his zummarah, lets loose with a Zulu war dance he

179

learned in Africa, and Mr. Perkins' poodle gets on her hind legs and waltzes, with tiny tottering steps.

Everyone is dancing?

Then what is that gentle snoring from the rustic arbor between the zebu yard and the zoril run? (I know I needn't pause to mention that zebus are Indian—East Indian, not Deerfoot and Gumbo Indian— oxen and zorils are African skunks.)

It is Caleb, of course. Caleb needs more excitement than brass bands, Indian war dances, and waltzing elephants to keep *him* awake.

Elephant, having finished his waltz, puts out his trunk, takes Mr. Kelly's cap, and puts it on his own head.

Everyone copies him.

Mr. Roberts, or Big Chief Lace War Bonnet, as his Indian friends still call him, from having seen Cousin Lucy's lace scarf bound around his raspberry-juice wounds, puts on Cousin Lucy's large lavender hat trimmed with lilacs, and Cousin Lucy puts on his new high silk hat.

Chimpanzee trades Mr. Roberts' old high silk hat for Jocko's round red cap.

Cousin Clement crowns Squaw Cooing Dove, the oldest lady present, with his carnation crown.

Aunt Bella wears Deerfoot's war bonnet, and he wears her garden hat tied under his chin with a blue bow.

Cousin Kate and Mud-on-His-Moccasins trade rainbow wig and medicine hat.

And so on.

Mud-on-His-Moccasins thinks that now he will be able to make rainbows, and is delighted, poor man.

Elephant ends by sinking to his knees in front of Mr. Kelly, and, just for fun, pretending to swoon with joy, and Apple slides to the ground in front of Cousin Clement.

Let's take hands and make a ring around them, to show how glad we are that they aren't lost any more.

You take Aunt Bella's hand, please. She takes Caleb's, with Squaw Cooing Dove next. Cooing Dove will keep even Caleb awake. Then Deerfoot, Aunt Ella, and Uncle Francis, carrying Fawnfoot, for a change for Fawnfoot and a treat for them both. Next, Gumbo, with Hotspur looking over his shoulder, not holding hoofs, but getting as close as he can, then the little Indian boy and I. Then Jocko, Cousin Kate, Mr. Kelly, Cousin Lucy, Medicine Man Mud-on-His-Moccasins, Mr. and Mrs. Noddy, Signor Olivetto, a little worried about Mrs. Noddy's fresh white kid gloves, for his hands are sticky from his orange, but exchanging smiles, bows, and Italian conversation. At least Signor Olivetto says quite a lot, and Mrs. Noddy smiles, bows, and says *"Grazia,"* which is Italian for "Thank you," isn't it? Mrs. Noddy isn't quite sure, and doesn't understand a word that Signor Olivetto is saying, but thinks that he is a charming gentleman, and he thinks that she is a charming lady. Signor Olivetto's other hand is held by Squaw Prickly Pear, who talks to him in the Indian language, and he doesn't understand a word that she is saying, but thinks that she is a charming lady, too. He hasn't had such a pleasant time since before Jocko took his holiday. Next to Prickly Pear comes Pinkfeather, then Mr. Perkins with his poodle and Quentin trying to sit on his feet, then Mr. Roberts, the Smiling Sultan, the taxi driver, the Terrible Turk, and Great-Uncle Thomas, with unga-puti (or agile gibbon) holding his hand with one paw and holding a vanilla ice-cream cone with the other paw, while her baby hangs around her neck.

"Now, how did she get out again?" murmurs Mr. Kelly to himself. "And where did she get that vanilla ice-cream cone?"

Winona, who gave it to her, holds the unga-puti's slender wrist with one hand and the wanderoo's paw with the other. The wanderoo has an ice-cream cone, too, but his is walnut. Then comes Wilhelmina, who let both the unga-puti and the wanderoo out. Then Aunt Winifred, Uncle Willie, Mr. Xiros, you—

Oh! We are back where we started. You begin and end the circle.

As we march around them, Apple makes a dancing school bow with his hand over his heart.

"Happy Birthday I've lost count of how many days ago, Cousin Clement. I've been trying to find you a Zebra butterfly to see, for your birthday present, but I couldn't, and I haven't—"

Since his hand is so near, he moves it gently up, to make sure that his friend and companion is still safe on his shoulder.

"—anything—"

Something is happening.

"—for—"

"Please, everyone, be still!" says Cousin Clement.

We are all still—so still that we can hear a faint creaking and squeaking in the cocoon. And I have only heard of one kind of butterfly that creaks and squeaks before it comes out.

The cocoon is moving.

The silk strands are breaking.

Caterpillar—or what had been Caterpillar when he went to sleep—comes slowly, clumsily out, a damp bedraggled body, with tiny rags of wings.

He moves slowly on Apple's shoulder; he stops to rest in the sunlight.

The damp, useless-looking wings are growing; you can see them grow.

Time passes; no one notices or cares. When Hotspur jingles his harness, everyone says "Sh-sh-sh—" like a sighing wind.

Now great, softly gleaming wings, marvelously streaked, lie folded over the slender body that has changed to dry, velvety fur. Long arched antennae spring from above big, shining eyes.

The wings open and fold, open and fold.

The butterfly rises in a short, fluttering flight, and lights on Apple's head.

Now it flies to Cousin Clement's hand.

182

Its wings are deep velvet-black, with a steel-blue sheen when the light catches them. Three stripes of bright yellow, like lightning at midnight, cross each upper wing; a broader yellow stripe runs across each lower wing, and under that shines a gentle curve of fourteen small yellow moons, and under the moons shine seven little yellow stars.

The tiny feet cling to Cousin Clement's hand. The wings close, and it is almost as though the butterfly vanished; no one would ever notice it. They open, and there are black midnight and yellow lightning and moons and stars.

"It is a Heliconius charitonius. It is a Zebra butterfly," Cousin Clement whispers. "The wish of my life has come true. I am seeing what I have longed to see. Appleby has brought me a Zebra butterfly."

Now the Zebra floats up, as though gentle zephyrs were blowing it toward the zenith.

Is it good-by?

No. Down again to Apple's hand, as though it could hardly bear to leave its companion and friend—then *up*!

Feasting and fun wait for Apple. Arms are outstretched, some wanting to hug him, some offering cake and ice cream. There will be presents from Great-Uncle Thomas, and traveler's tales to hear, and Apple will have some traveler's tales of his own to tell. There will be Winona and Wilhelmina, and probably the little Indian boy, to play with. Even now, Mr. Kelly is planning a fine reward to Apple for bringing Elephant back—his choice of the monkeys, maybe, or the privilege of feeding the lions, just as Aunt Ella, happily taking the blue wool, to remind her to find Apple, off her finger, is deciding that as soon as she has finished knitting the blue jacket for Jocko she will begin to knit a jacket for Elephant, to reward him for bringing Apple back—pink, so that it won't get mixed with Jocko's jacket. And Quentin is dropping the shining stone, the treasure Apple never expected to see again, at his feet.

It is going to be a happy time.

But now Apple can only look up to where his friend soars higher and higher into the bright blue sky.

"Good-by, Caterpillar!" he calls. "Good-by, beautiful butterfly! Good-by! I'll never forget you!"

HERE
IS THE STORY OF
APPLEBY CAPPLE.
NOBODY EVER HAS
HEARD IT
BEFORE.
HE GETS LOST, SO PLEASE
COME, WE'LL GO HUNTING FOR
APPLE,
JUST LIKE ALL HIS RELATIONS,
AND MANY ONES MORE.
NIGHT FALLS, WOODS
GROW DARK, BUT PERHAPS
YOU CAN FIND
HIM